CRYSTAL OF
STORMS

Fighting Fantasy: dare you play them all?

1. The Warlock of Firetop Mountain
2. City of Thieves
3. The Citadel of Chaos
4. The Forest of Doom
5. House of Hell
6. The Port of Peril
7. Creature of Havoc
8. Deathtrap Dungeon
9. Appointment with F.E.A.R.
10. Island of the Lizard King
11. Sorcery! 1: The Shamutanti Hills
12. The Gates of Death
13. Caverns of the Snow Witch
14. Sorcery! 2: Kharé: Cityport of Traps
15. Assassins of Allansia
16. Return to Firetop Mountain
17. Crystal of Storms

CRYSTAL OF
STORMS

RHIANNA
PRATCHETT

SCHOLASTIC

N

CONTENTS

Published in the UK by Scholastic Children's Books, 2020
Euston House, 24 Eversholt Street, London, NW1 1DB, UK
A division of Scholastic Limited.

London – New York – Toronto – Sydney – Auckland
Mexico City – New Delhi – Hong Kong

Text and illustrations © Ian Livingstone and Steve Jackson, 2020
Written by Rhianna Pratchett
Cover and inside illustrations by Eva Eskelinen, 2020

ISBN 978 1407 19968 9

A CIP catalogue record for this book is available from the British Library.

Printed by CPI Group (UK) Ltd, Croydon, CR0 4YY
Papers used by Scholastic Children's Books are made
from wood grown in sustainable forests.

1 3 5 7 9 10 8 6 4 2

www.scholastic.co.uk

Official FIGHTING FANTASY website: www.fightingfantasy.com

To Mum and Dad.
Who showed me magic every day.

HOW WILL YOU START
YOU ADVENTURE?

The book you hold in your hands is a gateway to another world – a world of dark magic, terrifying monsters, brooding castles, treacherous dungeons and untold danger, where a noble few defend against the myriad schemes of the forces of evil. Welcome to the world of **FIGHTING FANTASY**!

You are about to embark upon a thrilling fantasy adventure in which **YOU** are the hero! **YOU** decide which route to take, which dangers to risk and which creatures to fight. But be warned – it will also be **YOU** who has to live or die by the consequences of your actions.

Take heed, for success is by no means certain, and you may well fail in your mission on your first attempt. But have no fear, for with experience, skill and luck, each new attempt should bring you a step closer to your ultimate goal.

Prepare yourself, for when you turn the page you will enter an exciting, perilous **FIGHTING FANTASY** adventure where every choice is yours to make, an adventure in which **YOU ARE THE HERO**!

How would you like to begin your adventure?

IF YOU ARE NEW TO FIGHTING FANTASY . . .

It's a good idea to read through the rules which appear on pages 255-262 before you start.

IF YOU HAVE PLAYED FIGHTING FANTASY BEFORE . . .

You'll realize that to have any chance of success, you will need to discover your hero's attributes. You can create your own character by following the instructions on pages 269–276. Don't forget to enter your character's details on the Adventure Sheet which appears on page 278.

Also note that, unlike other Fighting Fantasy Gamebooks, in this adventure you do not start with any Provisions. Also please note the new rules on testing your *SKILL* and *STAMINA* on page 275.

ALTERNATIVE DICE

If you do not have a pair of dice handy, dice rolls are printed throughout the book at the bottom of the pages. Flicking rapidly through the book and stopping on a page will give you a random dice roll. If you need to 'roll' only one die, read only the first printed die; if two, total the two dice symbols.

BACKGROUND

The tempest children of Pangara, God of the Wind, have long reigned over the waters between Allansia and Khul. Many who sought to cross the perilous Ocean of Tempests have lost their lives to the raging storms or the terrifying sea creatures that dwell there. But deep within Zephyrus, largest of all the tempests, where the air is sweet and calm, lies the floating archipelago of Pangaria. The five islands of Cirrus, Altos, Cumulus, Incus and Asperitas surround a sixth small island known as Nimbus.

You were born and raised in Pangaria, but whilst many of your friends have opted to join the working communities of their home isles, such as Cloudkin farming on the water island of Altos or wrangling the magical (yet tasty) fauna of Cirrus, you dreamed bigger. You didn't want to settle for just one island. You wanted to see it all. And so you decided to join the Sky Watch, the guardians of peace within the whole of Pangaria. But your beloved home has a lot of peace to go around, and your first few weeks in the Sky Watch have been a rather dull parade of lost pets and mediating petty squabbles regarding overgrown shrubs. Your heart cries out for adventure.

And then one fine morning, an urgent message arrives at your Watchhouse summoning all the Sky Watch to an emergency meeting in the Citadel on Nimbus. It seems that adventure has finally listened and answered your plea.

Full of nervous excitement, your entire Watchhouse boards the local flyer – one of the small airships that transport Pangarians between islands. No one seems to know the purpose of the meeting, but it is bound to be something quite extraordinary for the entire Sky Watch to be summoned. You've only been to the Citadel once, when you were sworn into the Sky Watch, and it still holds newness and excitement for you. Stretching, you lean your head out of the flyer window and crane your neck in order to get the first glimpse of the towering spires and sculpted ramparts of the Citadel, the home of Pangaria's lawmakers, diplomats and island officials. The flyer's Goblin pilot wearily reminds you to keep all limbs inside the ship, lest you lose something essential.

Although you've heard tell that there are tribes of Goblins out in the world who are aggressive towards humans and other species, the Goblins of Pangaria are largely friendly. Most importantly, they developed the technomancy – a blend of elemental magic and engineering – that keeps Pangaria airborne.

You're just about to disembark and take your first steps

on to Nimbus when your commander, Captain Halleck, looks aghast. "By Zephyrus's breath!" he exclaims, looking directly at you. "I've forgotten my hovers! Can't be seen in the Citadel without those. Please retrieve them from the Watchhouse, recruit." He pats at his pockets, searching for something. "Bring my coin bag too."

You nod. As the newest member of your Watchhouse, you don't really have a choice. Remaining on board the flyer as the rest of the Watch disembarks, you hope you can get there and back without missing anything exciting. Seeing your frustration, the flyer's pilot softens and cranks up the craft to its top speed and brings you right up to the Watchhouse door. You rush inside and soon return, clutching the small leather purse, jingling with coins, and carrying Halleck's hovers.

Up close you can't help but marvel at the intricate, light-as-air metalwork of these portable wings, powered by storm crystals, harvested and gathered from the local tempest by the elemental Stormborns. You look forward to the day when you are senior enough to get your own pair. You check the crystal gauge, which is attached to a small blue-green storm crystal that has a tiny imprisoned tempest swirling inside it. It's a third full, but there's no time to charge the wings. You throw yourself back into the flyer.

The little airship has barely had time to set down when you leap from the bulwark and start to sprint towards the Citadel. Suddenly a great explosion rocks Nimbus and a wave of energy surges outwards from the fortress, catapulting you through the air and over the edge of the island.

You begin to plummet downwards.

YOUR ADVENTURE AWAITS!

May your STAMINA never fail!

NOW TURN OVER...

1

The explosion has knocked the wind out of you. There's only one thing you can do to save yourself as you tumble through the howling air. You manage to struggle into Halleck's hovers, and the wings unfold with a soft *thwack, thwack, thwack* sound. Your fall ceases as the hovers slow your descent and hold you aloft. Your relief turns to fear as you look up and realize that now it's Nimbus which is falling. Straight towards you.

Using your shoulder muscles to operate the hovers, you manage to steer yourself out of the path of the falling island as it hurtles past, tossing you around like a feather on the breeze. You gain control only to see Nimbus crashing into the sea far below. You watch in horror as the island begins to sink beneath the waves.

You become aware of an unsettling humming sound and the wings begin to shudder. The crystal that powers the hovers must be running out of charge! There's just enough power left to fly you to the safety of your home island.

If your home island is Cirrus, the farming island, turn to **84**. If your home island is Altos, the water island, turn to **196**. If your home island is Cumulus, the island of trade, turn to **298**.

2

It's time to look somewhere else.

To charge your hovers and fly to Asperitas, the isle of technomancy, turn to **384**.

If you do not have any Gold Pieces, you can continue no further and your adventure is over.

3

You glide the *Barnacle* down to the outskirts of Nimbus. The flowers and gardens look like exotic coral reefs. As you are trying to remember how to get to the main entrance of the Citadel, you spot another brass sphere. It's another bathysphere, only this one is stuck in the trees and has a great gash in its side. It must be the *Barracuda*, the sphere that never returned when Nimbus crashed.

If you want to investigate the other bathysphere, turn to **393**. If you want to continue to the Citadel, turn to **290**.

4

"Well, I mean, Nimbus falling, of course! It's all anyone's talking about."

If you want to ask him why he thought you might believe he's involved, turn to **116**. If you want to lie and accuse him of being behind it, turn to **372**.

5

You show Methedus the storm crystal shard and explain how you came by it. A strange expression crosses his face which you can't quite read. He studies the object, running his translucent hands over its faceted surface.

"This isn't like any crystal I've ever seen before. It's

large; not as large as the ones that power the islands, but too big to be used in hovers or flyers."

He touches the marks on the inner side of the crystal.

"These marks are where the crystal's energy must have broken out. Become unstable. Whatever happened to this one, it was broken from the inside out. The black residue on the outside is some kind of oil. That's all I can tell you for now. I must continue my work inside. There is bread to be made. Good day to you."

He hands the storm crystal shard back to you.

If you feel like you've heard all you need to, turn to **205**. If you think he's hiding something and want to secretly follow him, turn to **121**.

6

You give Vizigg the black candle. "Hmm, it's more of a dark grey colour, but it'll do," he says, taking it from you.

If you have a copper ring, turn to **228**. If you have a silver goblet, turn to **115**. If you want to leave the Under-Library and go in search of these items, turn to **26**. If you have given Vizigg all the requested items, turn to **206**.

7

You manage to dodge the incoming globule, but you still have to deal with whatever launched it. A Giant Toad waddles out of the swamp, blocking your path. It readies itself to launch another gloopy missile in your direction.

To fight the creature, turn to **44**. If you have a Calming Potion and want to use it now, turn to **204**.

8

The Goblin flyer brings you safely to Incus, the fishing island. You try to recall what you know about the island. Unlike the other residents of the archipelago, the Incus fishermen have been granted direct access to the Ocean of Tempests by Pangaria's authorities. Incus also floats lower than the other islands, which makes this easier. Various craft are built and used by the Incus islanders to trawl the ocean, bringing fresh fish, seaweed, coral, shells and other sea-born bounties to the lands above. The craft are embedded with storm crystals which allow them to fly up and down from Incus as required.

Due to the protective arms of the giant Zephyrus Tempest, the section of ocean directly under the archipelago is usually a calm and rich fishing ground. The main dangers are the larger and more ferocious aquatic creatures who share these waters. Only the hardy can survive the Ocean of Tempests and they are best left well alone.

However, the needs of a civilization, even a small one like Pangaria, are varied, and so the fishermen of Incus must often venture beyond the Zephyrus Tempest and into the wider ocean. There the rougher seas require sub-aquatic craft known as bathyspheres which can hunt and gather below the waves, although they are noisier and more cumbersome, and therefore run a greater risk of disturbing the local fauna.

Incus also receives limited trade from trusted sources on the mainland, although the islanders are careful not to let them set foot on the archipelago. Very occasionally Pangarian fishermen have rescued shipwreck survivors from the waters. If those survivors require aid that cannot be administered by the fishermen themselves, they are taken to Pangaria, and given aid and sanctuary. Permanent sanctuary. Keeping the secrets of Pangaria safe is one of the first rules that every islander learns.

You disembark. If the codeword **Galen** is on your Adventure Sheet, turn to **337**. Otherwise, turn to **90**.

9

You head towards the kitchen. You listen at the big iron-studded door, and hear a dull *moaning* coming from inside. Another creature, perhaps? A terrible monster? The walking dead? You shove open the door forcefully, readying yourself to meet whatever horrors await you on the other side. Turn to **188**.

Human and cephalopod have become one

Looking around carefully to check that no one is watching, you clamber into the hammock.

Its gentle movement soon rocks you to sleep. You dream of floating metal eyeballs following your every movement and a giant metal hand reaching down from the storm clouds to crush you. You awaken feeling refreshed (restore up to 3 *STAMINA* points) but then suddenly find yourself roughly jerked out of the hammock. You go to pick yourself up off the floor and see a pair of black boots in front of you.

Expecting to look up at the enraged fisherman whose hammock you've been caught napping in, you're horrified to find yourself face-to-face with a large, pulsating Octopus. Pulling yourself upright, you realize that you were half right, the Octopus is attached to a man's head, completely obscuring his skull. Its body crackles with elemental energy and its tentacles are wrapped around the man's torso and arms. Human and cephalopod have become one – one hulking, enraged creature that has you in its sights.

OCTOMAN	SKILL 10	STAMINA 10

Once you reduce the Octoman's *STAMINA* score to 5 points or fewer, turn to **106** at once.

11

You ask Vizigg about his condition. He looks down at his blood- and dust-covered robes. "I got pinned under some masonry during the fall. Crawled out eventually. But I doubt I'm long for this world."

If you want to ask him why the Nimbus crashed and haven't already, turn to **82**. If you want to ask what Vizigg is doing with the broken storm crystals and haven't already, turn to **59**. If you want to ask about the ward on the Great Hall and haven't already, turn to **338**. If you are done asking him questions, turn to **170**.

12

You aim for a soft-looking haystack and, just as the wings of your hovers are starting to fold up, you drop safely into the soft, warm hay. A grazing mule gently nuzzles you to your feet.

If Cumulus is your home isle, turn to **57**. If Cumulus is not your home isle, turn to **88**.

13

You keep up with the flying eye with ease. Turn to **38**.

14

The light dims and the sea creature sinks to the bottom of the cave. You look around the rocky ledge and see that the Wraithfish was quite the hoarder. There are lots of metallic bits and pieces strewn around the cave.

You root around amongst the junk to see if you can uncover anything of value. You find a strange brass rod, which looks like it might have come from a boat, and a silver goblet. (Add both these items to your Equipment List.)

You manage to get the *Barnacle* back into the water. The craft still looks useable, despite everything it's been through. You get back in and decide where to go next.

If you have the codeword **Rescue** recorded on your Adventure Sheet, you can turn to **132**. If not, and you want to leave the passage and take the left fork in the caves, if you haven't explored that way already, turn to **231**. To leave the caves and head for the large dim shape, turn to **191**.

15

You have the key to your own chest, whilst another has caught Silas's attention. Checking the rest, you discover that one is unlocked.

If you want to search your chest, turn to **217**. If you want to open the unlocked chest, turn to **65**. If you want to see what Silas has found, turn to **134**.

16

You throw the trident to Tideus. (If you are currently using the trident, you must switch to a different weapon.)

"Now dat is wot I calls a weapon," he bellows delightedly.

He hurls the trident at the Goblin War Golem, hitting the ungodly metal creation in what passes for its chest. (Deduct 5 points from the War Golem's *STAMINA* score.)

"Pah!" shouts Krazic. "It's going to take more than a little sea fork to stop us!" Turn to **326**.

17

You tell Caleb about your investigations and ask him to tell you more about this *Doombringer*.

"It was a few weeks back," explains Caleb. "Great big vessel. Got caught between a couple of tempests. Nasty business. Rescued one survivor, but the ship sank like a stone."

He starts to cough again.

To ask more about the survivor, turn to **281**. To ask if there's anything else Caleb knows about the *Doombringer*, turn to **33**. To leave him and continue to the east dock, turn to **295**.

The lower areas of the library are waist deep in water. Books float by in shoals. The upper levels are dry, though, so you make your way there.

You wade between the shelves. Suddenly you hear strange noises coming from . . . well, you don't quite know where. It sounds like *chanting*, with the occasional *shuffling* and *banging* sound. You follow the sound and it takes you to a section of bookshelf. The sound is coming from directly behind it.

You check the bookshelf for handles. Then you study the books carefully. You notice that there are four dotted across the shelves that have very similar spines. You decide to reach for one to see if it will help solve this conundrum. Do you reach for:

*Tooth and Claw: Famous Fights to
the Death?*   Turn to **45**.
Winged Menaces: Death from Above?   Turn to **89**.
*A Sting in the Tale: A Collection of
Unexpected Endings?*   Turn to **239**.
*Denizens of the Deep: Aquatic Beasts and
How to Kill Them?*   Turn to **341**.

If you don't want to pick up any of the books, then there's nowhere else to explore in the library and so turn to **92** to return to the Nimbiferous Chamber.

19

You tell Nix you don't think it's a good idea for him to be doing this.

"This thing half destroyed my workshop," he grumbles. "I want to see it gone! Or at least moved. Once it's off my property, it's all yours, Officer."

You reluctantly agree and let Nix charge up the boulder. Lose 1 *LUCK* point and **250**.

20

You give him the supposed cure and tell him that it might help with his current condition. He sniffs it closely.

"You know, I think you're right," Kritch says cheerfully. "Give it a few minutes to work and I'm sure I'll be up to piloting the flyer. I'm only licenced to take you to Incus. Take the north flyer port from there for Asperitas. If you want to visit Cirrus or Cumulus, you'll need to use your hovers."

If you want to charge up your hovers for 1 Gold Piece and fly to Cirrus or Cumulus, turn to **96**. If you'd like to take the flyer to Incus, the fishing island, turn to **8**.

21

You attempt to break down the door but you just end up jarring your shoulder. (Lose 2 *STAMINA* points and 1 *SKILL* point.) The locking system behind it must be incredibly strong.

If you want to head west, towards where the residents

of Asperitas live, turn to **293**. Alternatively, you can head north, deeper into the maze of workshops and laboratories – turn to **111**.

22

You tell the fisherman that you'll do what you can to help him. With that, you guide the bathysphere beneath the waves. Turn to **203**.

23

You hold the lemon-drenched page up to the light. As it heats up, a mess of brown appears. If there was something written on there, you can't read it. But it's clear that Vizigg must have been sending and receiving secret messages. Unfortunately, there's nothing more you can do about it now.

You leave the tower and head north-east into the maze of workshops and laboratories. Turn to **111**.

24

You say that honestly, you don't know, but you're doing everything you can to find out what caused the explosion and hopefully find a way to restore Nimbus. Maude gives you the hard stare, weighing up what you said. Turn to **364**.

25

You hurl the Calming Potion towards Flapps, who grabs it in his teeth. The bottle breaks and the liquid pours into his mouth. It works quickly and Flapps starts to shrink in size. The glow leaves his eyes and his fur stops sparking.

Flapps shakes his head and looks confused. Then he bounds forward and covers both you and Nemi in wet licks.

"OK, boy, OK. Enough! Enough!" laughs Nemi, stroking Flapps's fur. "You go back to the farm and wait for me there."

Flapps barks, bounds out of the cave and takes off, heading for the Cloudkin farm.

"Thank you for that," says Nemi. "If Flapps had been left much longer, he'd have been beyond saving." (Gain 1 *LUCK* point.)

She rummages in the dirt at the back of the cave. "Hmm, what's this?"

She picks up a longsword and dusts it off.

"You take it," she says. "A thank you from me and Flapps."

(Record the longsword on your Adventure Sheet. If you

use the longsword in battle, you may increase your Attack Strength by 1 point.)

"Oh, and here." Nemi's eagle eyes have spotted something else in the cave. She passes you 2 Gold Pieces. (Record these on your Adventure Sheet as well.)

If you want to investigate the Goblin flyer, turn to **361**. If you haven't been to the Watchhouse and want to go there now, turn to **40**.

26

You decide that you need to explore a bit more.

If you decide to go back to the bathysphere, turn to **136**. If you want to go back to the Nimbiferous Chamber, turn to **194**.

27

You follow the signs towards where you would expect to find Cumulus's Goblin flyer, but as you near the dock, you can see no sign of it. At first you think it must be traversing one of its routes, but then you hear a plaintive "Help! Help! Anyone? *Anyone?*"

You peer over the edge of the dock and see the Goblin pilot hanging off the edge of some rocks below. The Goblin looks very relieved to see you. "Could you possibly give me a hand here?"

You pull the Goblin to safety and she introduces herself as Daxa.

"That Nimbus explosion completely took out my flyer," she explains. "Blew it right down into the ocean. Luckily, I managed to jump out when I did, or I'd probably be in some Great White Squark's belly by now!"

You explain that you were hoping to visit the other islands.

"Well, until I get another flyer, you won't be able to get to Incus or Asperitas," Daxa says, sadly. "But I'll charge your hovers for free and that will get you to Cirrus or Altos. You can take the flyers from there."

She points to a long bridge nearby, half shrouded in clouds.

"Normally you could take the Sky Bridge to Cirrus, but it's been closed due to some unnatural disturbances around the bridge at this end," Daxa explains. "Of course, if you can deal with that, I'd be happy to reopen it, especially as my best aeronaut's helmet got thrown there during the crash. If you can make the bridge safe again, then the helmet is yours."

If you want Daxa to charge your flyers for free and fly to Altos, turn to **342**. If you want Daxa to charge your flyers for free and fly to Cirrus, turn to **320**. If you want to investigate the Sky Bridge to Cirrus and see if you can find the aeronaut's helmet, turn to **233**.

28

You run forward and sweep up the elderly Goblin, managing to save both of you from the falling debris. Turn to **216**.

29

You pick up the sketches and realize with a shiver that they're drawings of you. There's one of you sleeping at the Cirrus Watchhouse, and another of you walking around Asperitas.

You can also see notes detailing your movements around the islands. Whoever lives in this house has been very interested in what you've been up to.

You're filled with rage. You look at the contraption charging the Eye-Spies and see that it regulates the level of charge the storm crystals are receiving.

Do you want to try to overload the charge and destroy the Eye-Spies (turn to **389**), or would you prefer to explore the ground floor, if you haven't already done so (turn to **182**)? Alternatively, you can leave the house by turning to **149**.

*An enormous black Cloudkin floats
out from behind one of the farm buildings*

You head towards the farm. This is where the Cloudkin are born and raised when young, before they are let out to roam in the skies above Altos, the Zephyrus Tempest preventing them from drifting too far away. There they grow fat with rain and are cared for at ground level by Altos's many farmers and in the air by Canidors – winged, dog-like creatures.

Any island that needs rain or shade can request a herd of Cloudkin, which will come to the island and deposit their rain before returning to Altos to be fattened up again. Cloudkin are usually gentle and passive, aside from protective mothers, as you just found out.

But as you get nearer, the farm seems unusually quiet. There are no workers outside, or Canidors in the air, and there are even a few discarded tools lying about. A chill goes down your spine. Something bad has happened here.

Suddenly, there's a *thunderous growl*. An enormous black Cloudkin floats out from behind one of the farm buildings, lightning sparking from within its swirling dark depths. This is like no Cloudkin you've ever seen before. The energy from the Nimbus must have mutated it from a benign rain cloud into an angry ball of storm energy.

"Here! Take this!" You turn to see a young woman dressed in waterproof farming clothes. She throws you a Cloudkin staff – a special staff used in the farming of the sentient clouds. (Add the Cloudkin staff to your Adventure Sheet.)

"Let's subdue this storm!" she shouts over the rumbling, thunderous growls of the Stormkin.

With this woman fighting with you for the duration of this battle, you may add 2 points when calculating your Attack Strength, you may increase any damage you cause by 1 point, and you may reduce any damage you suffer in battle by 1 point.

Together you can take on the Stormkin.

STORMKIN 　　　　*SKILL 10* 　　　　*STAMINA 10*

If you win, and Altos is your home island, turn to **353**. If you win, but Altos is not your home island, turn to **277**.

You are just about to take a dive into the water when Nemi pulls you back.

"What are you doing, you idiot?" she yells at you. "Don't you see the colour of the water?"

You look down again. The water does look darker than you remember, and not its usual beautiful azure blue.

Perhaps diving in isn't such a great idea after all. A scaly backbone cuts the surface of the water briefly before disappearing. Yes, definitely not a good idea.Turn to **75**.

32

You fight your way through the angry vines until they retreat away from the door, giving you enough time to escape. You notice a bunch of unexploded grapes lying on the floor. You prod them very gently with your sword, but they seem more stable when not connected to the vine. It will take more force to activate their corrosive properties. Thinking they might come in useful, you carefully put them in a small leather pouch and take them with you. (Add the corrosive grapes to your Adventure Sheet.)

You leave the Watchhouse and are just wondering if you should go to the north of Cirrus and locate a Goblin flyer to take you onwards to the other islands when you hear an indistinct yelling in the distance.

If you want to follow the sound of the yelling, turn to **168**. If you want to investigate the plume of blue-green smoke, turn to **137**. If you want to head north, turn to **255**.

33

You ask Caleb if there's anything more he can tell you about the *Doombringer*.

"It was a warship. Weapons. Cannons. Not sure where it was heading, but all that metal made it sink like a stone. Guess we'll never know now. There's always a war going on some place. Folks love a good fight. Give me the peace of Pangaria any day!"

To leave Caleb and continue your journey, turn to **295**. If you haven't asked more about the survivor already, turn to **281**.

34

You duck and roll as a blade swishes over your head. You might have got a slight haircut, but otherwise you're unharmed. You wonder why anywhere in the Citadel would need such a trap to protect it.

You're still wondering this as you walk forward and get slightly scorched by a fireball spat out by a statue embedded in the wall. (Lose 1 *STAMINA* point.)

Make that traps.

You move ahead extremely cautiously. Turn to **210**.

35

With the queen dead, the other Cockroaches quickly withdraw from your sight. You search the room, picking your way around the foul-smelling corpse. You don't find your own Gold Bag, but you do find another with 3 more Gold Pieces in than you had when your own bag was taken. (Update this on the Gold Box on your Adventure Sheet.) You also find a small jar of healing honey and some dried fish. (Add these to your Adventure Sheet. The healing honey will restore up to 3 *STAMINA* points and the dried fish will give you 2 *STAMINA* points.)

Climbing on top of the Queen Cockroach's corpse, you are able to reach the hole in the roof. You pull yourself out and head back to your adventures, a little heavier and a little smellier. Turn to **336**.

36

With the crystal's warning alarm ringing in your ears, you manage to steer the hovers gently down to Cirrus. The wings fold up behind you as you stare across to where Nimbus used to be. Now there's nothing but air and dust, which crackles with a strange energy. Whatever brought the island down must've been incredibly powerful. Turn to **321**.

You move your bathysphere closer to the bubble. The figure inside is ethereal and translucent. You realize it's one of the Stormborn.

"Ah, you're still alive!" he grins. "I hoped you would be. My name is Methedus." You realize that Matix's amplification device is allowing you to hear him perfectly, even inside the bathysphere.

"The path you travel will not be an easy one," the Stormborn continues. "I thought this might come in handy."

And with that Methedus waves his hands and creates a small bubble in which floats a Potion of Power. He pushes the little bubble through the walls of his own and floats it across to the *Barnacle*, where you can capture it. (Add the Potion of Power to your Adventure Sheet. This will increase your Attack Strength by 2 points for the duration of one fight only and restore 3 *STAMINA* points as well.)

You ask him why the Stormborn haven't helped the Nimbus.

"Alas, a ward has been placed around Nimbus which prevents any Stormborn from getting close. But I should warn you that I believe there to be another Stormborn still inside. What his role is in all this chaos I do not know for sure, but be careful. It's up to you now, Officer."

With that, Methedus and his bubble float back to the surface. Turn to **3**.

38

You observe the flying eye zipping into a small hatch in the side of a ramshackle wooden house. You have no idea who it belongs to. Do you want to:

Knock on the front door of the house? Turn to **102**.

Quietly go round to the back of the house and see if you can find another way in? Turn to **287**.

39

You hurl the giant Crab Pincher towards the Goblin War Golem. "Oh!" says Tideus. "A snack! Tideus likes snacks!"

As he makes a grab for the pincer, Krazic takes advantage of the distraction and cracks the Sea Giant across the head with his stone club.

(Deduct 3 *STAMINA* points and 1 *SKILL* points from the Sea Giant.) Turn to **326**.

40

You set off for the Watchhouse, taking the most direct route through an expanse of marshy land, whilst wondering who might still be left there, and why they missed the meeting on Nimbus. As you ponder this, you hear a low rumbling sound. Fearing it might be another Stormkin, you ready your weapon. Suddenly a globule of sticky goo flies through the air straight towards you.

Test Your Luck. If you are Lucky, turn to **7**. If you are Unlucky, turn to **397**.

41

You urge the *Barnacle* forward, preparing to engage the creature in combat.

GIANT ELECTRIC EEL   SKILL 8   STAMINA 8

Every three Attack Rounds, the Eel will emit a pulse of electricity that will cause 3 *STAMINA* points of damage to the bathysphere, whether you wound the creature or not.

If you win the battle, turn to **172**. However, if you lose the battle, the battered *Barnacle* sinks to the bottom of the ocean, condemning you to a slow death.

42

Thankfully, the stairs leading to the upper level are still intact, even though part of the floor has collapsed. Like downstairs, there are no signs of life and it looks like a storm has blown through the place.

If you want to explore further, turn to **274**. If you want to leave and go towards Matix's home, turn to **161**. If you want to leave and head to the east dock and the bathysphere shed, turn to **74**.

43

You return to Halleck in the room below. You don't want to alarm him, so you make sure he's comfortable and tell him you're going to continue searching the Citadel.

"Good work, Officer!" Halleck says, saluting you.

If you have the codeword **Nimbi** on your Adventure Sheet, turn to **92**. If not, turn to **347**.

44

You square up to the Giant Toad, preparing to battle it to the death. For one of you at least.

GIANT TOAD   *SKILL 5*   *STAMINA 7*

If you win, turn to **181**.

45

You gingerly take down *Tooth and Claw: Famous Fights to the Death.* The book jumps out of your hand, the pages flipping back and forth. Claws come out of the page, followed by muscular, hairy arms, and then an entire Clawbeast emerges from the enchanted tome, hungry for a fight.

CLAWBEAST   *SKILL 9*   *STAMINA 14*

If you win, turn to **263**.

46

On entering the mill, you can see that the circle Methedus was floating above is covered in strange symbols. You ask what exactly he's doing, fearing that he may somehow be involved in the fall of the Nimbus.

"When the explosion happened, there was a Stormborn present," he explains. "I felt their energy and I also felt it leave after the Nimbus fell. Perhaps they were there when it happened and fled from the scene, or maybe they're trapped down there, I don't know. I was trying to reconnect with their energy, but no matter what I do, I can't. Or I couldn't until I touched that shard you brought me. It has the same energy."

You ask him what he means by that.

"You may not know this, but each storm crystal is intrinsically imprinted with the mark of its maker. These are invisible to all but other Stormborns. The shard you had was made by a Stormborn called Boreas. He's an elder of our tribe, but he's not been seen for a while. It pains me to admit this of another Stormborn, but Boreas is involved somehow."

He's telling the truth; you can feel it in your bones.

Methedus passes you a small crystal. It looks like a blank version of the one you have in your hovers.

"You might need this, Officer. You seem like the type that gets themselves into danger. There are a lot of nasty energies around and this will remove them from an infected creature, just as long as it's not too far gone. Once the animal has been taken over entirely, the crystal won't work. One use only, I'm afraid." (Add Methedus's shard to your Adventure Sheet and 1 point to your *LUCK* score.)

Add the codeword **Boreas** to your Adventure Sheet, if you haven't already.

There's nothing more left to do here.

If you want to look for Hazi in the market, and haven't done so already, turn to **351**. If you want to find the local Goblin flyer and head on for the other islands, turn to **27**.

47

You finish off the Octobeast before it can infect anyone else. But now you urgently need to return to your investigations.

If you have the codeword **Renard** written on your Adventure Sheet, turn to **56**.

If not, where do you want to go now? To head north towards Matix's home, turn to **161**. To head to the east dock and the bathysphere workshop, turn to **74**.

48

You speedily make your way back to the Nimbiferous Chamber.

If you'd rather investigate in the kitchens, turn to **9**. If you've not yet tried to open the Great Hall door, turn to **369**.

You head for the Watchhouse. There must be something you can scavenge there.

You're passing by a field of gently waving corn when you become aware of a growing *chittering* sound. The sound gets louder and louder as more creatures join in. The stalks begin to ripple as something surges towards you and erupts out of the corn.

It's a horde of Corn Rats. These usually peaceful pests have been aggravated by the surge of energy from the explosion on Nimbus and have ditched their regular vegetarian diet for something a little meatier – you!

RABID RAT HORDE *SKILL 6* *STAMINA 10*

If you win, turn to **109**.

The elemental energy hasn't completely corrupted him

50

The shadow unfolds a pair of wings. As it draws closer, you can see it's a Canidor – or at least it was once. Now it's fighting the effects of the surge of elemental energy from the explosion. Its eyes glow with flashes of lightning, while sparks crackle off its fur.

You can see a collar around its neck. The name tag reads *Flapps*.

Flapps snarls, revealing wickedly sharp teeth. Then he *whimpers* a little. The elemental energy hasn't completely corrupted him, but it can't be long before it does.

If you want to use a Calming Potion on Flapps, turn to **285**. If you have Methedus's Shard and want to use it on Flapps, turn to **265**. If you want to fight Flapps, turn to **147**. If you want to flee, hoping the Canidor doesn't pursue you, and head for the Goblin flyer instead, turn to **361**.

51

You press your storm crystal to the larger shard. A force of energy knocks you back. Luckily Silas catches you. (Lose 2 *STAMINA* points.)

"Looks like that crystal's too volatile to charge from," says Silas, helping you up.

You break off a small piece of the shard near one of the cracks and examine it. Strangely, the damage seems to be on the inside of the crystal. You can see worn grooves and cracks on the inside and a strange black residue on the outside. (Record the storm crystal shard on your Adventure Sheet.)

Perhaps you can find someone who'll be able to tell you where the crystal came from and what broke it. Maybe then you'll be able to find out what happened on Nimbus.

If you want to visit the Watchhouse, if you haven't already, turn to **49**. If you want to investigate the shed, turn to **376**.

52

You return to Vizigg.

"Ah, it's you," he wheezes. "What do you have for me?"

If you have the copper ring for him, turn to **228**. If you have the silver goblet for him, turn to **115**. If you have the black candle for him, turn to **6**. If you want to leave the Under-Library to keep looking for any missing items, turn to **26**.

53

You tell Yurik that it was Pox who told you he was involved with the Nimbus crash.

"It's not true!" he squeaks. "I never trusted him, or Paxlo! Never! I don't know what them and the others were up to in Krazic's workshop on Nimbus, but they were being paid double to be there. Hush money if you ask me."

You decide to ask about the workshop. Turn to **133**.

You're glad to finally be on your way to Nimbus, but at the same time you're terrified of what you might find down there. Beyond the storms, is the Nimbus still afloat, or has it sunk into the ocean depths? Are any of your friends in the Sky Watch still alive?

The bathysphere shakes a little as it passes through the turbulent storm clouds, but soon you feel it land with a large splash in the water. Rain drums on the top of the bathysphere and the waves toss you from side to side, making you feel ill. The Ocean of Tempests is living up to its name.

From now on, unless you exit the bathysphere or you are specifically told to use your personal *SKILL* and *STAMINA* score, you must use the bathysphere's *SKILL* and *STAMINA* scores instead.

BATHYSPHERE   *SKILL (see below)*   *STAMINA 20*

The bathysphere's *SKILL* score is equal to your *Initial* SKILL score, minus 1.

Any bonuses or penalties you have as a result of using particular weapons do not apply for as long as you are using the bathysphere's *SKILL* and *STAMINA* score. (Make sure you continue to keep a careful record of your personal stats.) Now turn to **186**.

55

The shadow unfolds a pair of wings. As it gets closer you can see it's a Canidor, or rather was a Canidor. Now it's fighting the effects of the surge of elemental energy from the explosion. Its eyes glow with flashes of lightning and sparks are crackling off its fur.

"It's Flapps!" cries Nemi.

Flapps snarls, revealing wickedly sharp teeth.

"Good boy, easy, easy," whispers Nemi, soothingly. It's me."

Flapps whimpers a little. The elemental energy hasn't completely corrupted him, but it can't be long before it does.

"You have to find a way to help him," Nemi pleads with you.

If you have a Calming Potion and want to use it on Flapps, turn to **25**. If you want to turn back and head for the Goblin flyer instead, turn to **361**.

56

Where do you want to go now? Will you head:

To the Renard house?	Turn to **118**.
North towards Matix's home?	Turn to **161**.
To the east dock and the bathysphere workshop?	Turn to **74**.

57

57

The usual bustling sounds of the market are more muted today. You don't see as many stalls open, and the crowds are sparser than normal. The explosion on Nimbus has driven many indoors, but the stallholders are hardier, and most won't run and hide whilst there's even one person to make money from.

If you can charge up Halleck's hovers you will have a valuable piece of equipment at your disposal. You also realize you've managed to keep hold of his Coin Bag. He won't mind you borrowing it in the line of duty. (Add 10 Gold Pieces to your Adventure Sheet.)

You check your waist; your trusty short sword is still there, thankfully. You get the feeling you might need it. (Add this to your Adventure Sheet.)

"Whoa! Ain't you a little junior for those hovers?"

It's Dav, a Goblin friend of yours who works in the local bakery. You vainly try to explain what happened on Nimbus and why you have Halleck's hovers, but it's still all so confusing and you have no answers to his questions yet.

"Sounds like you've had quite the morning," says Dav sympathetically, passing you a ginger-cream horn, which makes you feel just a little bit better. (Restore 1 *STAMINA* point.)

"We all heard the explosion," continues Dav. "Never seen the market fall so quiet. Some folks hid. Don't blame 'em with all the extra elemental energy wafting around here. Most of the stalls stayed open. You know the types around here; they wouldn't budge unless the ground fell out from under them! Er, let's hope it doesn't come to that."

Your resolutely tell Dav that you're going to investigate what happened. "Probably best if I join you while you're on Cumulus," says the little Goblin. "I've done all my chores and you look like you could use the company. Plus, I got a few moves if anything gets a bit fighty. Oh, and here, this might come in handy." He tosses you a Healing Potion. (This will restore up to 4 *STAMINA* points when drunk.)

As long Dav is travelling with you, you may add 2 points when calculating your Attack Strength, you may increase any damage you cause by 1 point, and you may reduce any damage you suffer in battle by 1 point. (Make a note of this on your Adventure Sheet.)

"Right," says Dav, readying himself for adventure. "There's a Goblin I know called Hazi who lives on the far side of the market. He used to work at the Citadel on Nimbus. He might know something. And we could always go and talk to Methedus, the Stormborn who works over at the mill. He might know a thing or two about the elemental energy that got released.

"There are rumours that the explosion has stirred up some nasty critters." Dav taps a small dagger at his belt.

"Good job you got ol' Dav with you. But maybe you want to tool up first, or make some coin?"

If you want to head for Hazi's place on the far side of the market, turn to **351**. If you want to head to the mill, turn to **261**. If you want to check out the market stalls, turn to **258**. If you want to engage in a game of chance in the hope of increasing your gold, turn to **304**.

58

You try to deflect the fireball with the blade of your Short Sword. The fireball bounces off your sword on to your boot and sets fire to your foot. (Lose 2 *STAMINA* points.) By the time you've put out the flames, the strange eyeball has flown away up the chimney.

You can't shake the feeling that you're being watched. But there's no time to dwell on such things right now. There's nothing more to do here, so you leave the Watchhouse. Turn to **335**.

59

You ask the Elder Technomancer what he's trying to do with the broken storm crystals.

"A ritual of repair, of course! Unfortunately, it's been hard finding the right elements in this place. Hardly ideal conditions."

If you want to ask him why the Nimbus crashed, and you haven't already, turn to **82**. If you want to ask about the ward on the Great Hall door, and you haven't already, turn to **338**. If you want to ask what has befallen him, and you haven't already, turn to **11**. If you are done asking him questions, turn to **170**.

60

"Your guess is as good as ours," says the fisherman who gave you the pincer. "We lost a few good boats when the Nimbus came down. One of the bathyspheres too. We tried to reach them, but the waters became too choppy, and a huge storm came in, pushing us away from the island. We had to bring all the boats up as fast as possible."

You're curious to know what happened to the Nimbus after it landed in the water.

"It was still afloat when I brought my boat up," chimes in another fisherman. "But things down there were getting very dangerous. All this fog came in, and gale force winds. Never seen it that bad."

You decide to ask the fishermen how you can get down to the Nimbus, turn to **331**.

61

You quickly reverse the *Barnacle* back along the tunnel. Suddenly there's a *crunching* sound at the back of the bathysphere. (Deduct 2 *STAMINA* points from the *Barnacle*'s *STAMINA* score.)

You turn the *Barnacle* around and come face-to-face with an enormous Wraithfish. It is an abyssal horror, with a mouth full of needle-sharp teeth and an appendage, like a fishing rod, coming from atop its head, which emits a blinding light.

And it's not happy about being reversed into by a ball of metal and is now out for blood.

ENRAGED WRAITHFISH   SKILL 10   STAMINA 12

If you win, turn to **179**.

62

You give Matix the Strange Metal Object that fell off the flying contraption that was spying on you in the Cirrus Watchhouse.

"Ah, a Doobry!" she says, looking pleased. "I think this should work in place of a Wotsit. But I'll still need a Thingie. And, of course, if you do find a Wotsit on your travels, I'll give you something handy in return."

To charge your hovers and fly to Asperitas, the isle of technomancy, turn to **384**. If you do not have any Gold Pieces, you can continue no further and your adventure is over.

63

They've served you well, but now it's time to put your hovers to greater use. You pass them to Vizigg and ask if the storm crystal in them will suffice.

The Technomancer takes the crystal out of the hovers. "Yes! Yes! I think this will work!"

You watch him reassemble the items, adjusting their positions and angles carefully.

"Right!" he says. "Let's get this island moving! Better hold on to something. I'm not entirely sure what's going to happen!"

He steps into the middle of the circle, holds up his leathery Goblin hands and begins to chant. The objects rise into the air and begin to spin around Vizigg. Eventually the broken storm crystals rise too, and the circle of spinning objects opens out, enveloping them.

"It's working!" Vizigg shouts, before returning to his chanting.

You watch with amazement as the broken storm crystals become whole again, and in each one a speck of green light begins to grow until there is a miniature tempest enclosed within.

Now the storm crystals are restored, the Nimbus begins to shake. It's starting to move upwards. Some rubble dislodges and falls towards Vizigg.

Test Your Skill. If you are Successful, turn to **28**. If you are Unsuccessful, turn to **286**.

64

The mill is quiet when you reach it. Perhaps the workers were sent home after the explosion. You look up at the windmill. There's no breeze, so the sails are still. There's a loud *whooshing* sound and what looks like a mini cyclone emerges from the structure. Before you know it, you're flung on to the ground (lose 2 *STAMINA* points) and find yourself being pulled across the ground towards the swirling mass. Turn to **104**.

65

You wonder briefly why the chest has been left unlocked, but when you lift the lid, you find out. The chest bites down on your hand (lose 2 *STAMINA* points and 1 *SKILL* point) and starts to bark and growl at you. It snaps its lid aggressively. You notice that the chest belongs to Private Seacrest and remember what a trickster he was. You quietly curse him under your breath.

If you have a Calming Potion and want to use it now, cross it off your Equipment List and turn to **238**. If not, you are going to have to fight the Chest Creature.

CHEST CREATURE   *SKILL* 5   *STAMINA* 6

If you win turn to **238**.

66

At your killing blow, the beast goes belly-up. Do you want to:

Cut open the creature's stomach and see if
it's eaten anything interesting?   Turn to **219**.

Leave the corpse and head into the library?   Turn to **18**.

67

You turn your body and take a run at the door. THUNK! It bows but doesn't completely break (lose 2 *STAMINA* points). You try a solid kick and the door bursts open. You head inside to find the source of the snoring. Turn to **306**.

68

You enter the correct combination and the door swings open.

You're in Vizigg's home. It's a rather cluttered, but cosy, with a little fireplace and a rocking chair, but the Elder Technomancer doesn't seem to be here. You hear a noise and something winged drops down the chimney into the cold fireplace.

Do you want to attempt to hide behind some furniture (turn to **319**), or do you want to stand your ground, even though you have no idea what it might be (turn to **343**)?

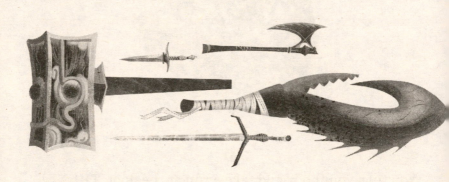

69

With an almighty crash, the Goblin War Golem finally topples. Metal body parts *clang* to the ground, the sound of the construct's destruction echoing around the Great

Hall. Boreas emerges from the chest cavity, severely weakened and defeated.

"What? Come back, you bag of wind!" Krazic screams from his seat inside the Golem's head, a prisoner once again. "What are you doing? Get back in here at once!"

But Boreas isn't listening anymore; he's more concerned with the winds that are springing up around him. His weakened state has destroyed the Stormborn ward surrounding Nimbus and now his elemental brethren are coming for him.

As the winds pick up, a dozen Stormborn appear around Boreas. He looks terrified as they descend on him. The storm grows to a crescendo and then abruptly dies back, leaving the Great Hall in silence, save for the odd Goblin cuss. The Stormborn have gone.

Halleck hobbles into the Great Hall, supported by Malia.

"Well done, Officer!" he says proudly. "You're a credit to the Sky Watch! Don't worry, we'll bring Krazic and his traitorous cronies to justice back in Pangaria."

You look out of the window to see that Nimbus is breaking the ocean's surface and taking to the skies once more. The water starts to drain from the Citadel, pouring back into the sea in beautiful salty waterfalls. And as it does so, the remaining survivors of the crash climb, hobble and crawl out of their hiding places, amazed at how you have saved them from a terrible fate. Turn to **400**.

There's an explosion of earth and rotting wood

70

You move carefully over the rooftops, looking for any sign of the creature. The *chittering* noise gets louder. Suddenly, a section of roof gives way under your feet and you drop down sharply, landing hard on the floor below. (Lose 3 *STAMINA* points.)

The hut you've dropped into is long abandoned, the floor half rotted away, and what remains is covered in dirt and viscous slime. Several Giant Cockroaches approach you, *hissing*; antennae waving angrily. There are far too many to take on at once.

There's a loud *screeching* sound and the Giant Cockroaches pull back. Something's coming that even they are frightened of. The ground starts to vibrate. There's an explosion of earth and rotting wood as a huge cockroach erupts from under the floor. At least you only have one target now.

COCKROACH QUEEN   *SKILL 7*   *STAMINA 7*

If you win, turn to **35**.

71

It's a glancing blow. The contraption emits a high-pitched noise, before flying away up the chimney.

You're unharmed but can't shake the feeling that you're being watched. But there's no time to dwell on such things right now, you need to get moving.

(Write the codeword **Eye-Spy** on your Adventure Sheet.)

Choosing something you've not already tried. Will you:

Search your chest?	Turn to **217**.
See what Silas found earlier?	Turn to **134**.
Leave the Watchhouse?	Turn to **335**.

72

The door looks quite flimsy. You square up to it.

Test Your Stamina, subtracting 2 from the dice roll if you have an axe or club-like weapon with you. If you pass the test, turn to **229**. If you fail the test, turn to **381**.

73

You reach the other side. You're soaking wet and your clothes feel heavy. You start to shiver (lose 1 *STAMINA* point). You notice some old papers and a broken chair nearby.

If you have some waterproof firesticks or a flask of fire oil, you can start a fire by turning to **124**. If you do not have either of these items, then turn to **288** to continue onwards.

You make your way towards the east dock in the hope of tracking down Matix at the bathysphere shed. It takes you an hour or so but when you eventually find it, your face falls. One of the large dockyard cranes has fallen on to the shed. You tell one of the dock workers that you need to commandeer a bathysphere to get down to the Nimbus.

"Well, *Anemone* and *Coral* are pinned under that crane," explains the worker. "It's going to take us a while to move it, and even then, both bathyspheres will need repairs before they're operational again."

You ask what's happened to the other two bathyspheres.

"We lost contact with *Barracuda* shortly after the Nimbus fell, and Matix has been working on *Barnacle* over at her home workshop for a few weeks now. If you need a bathysphere, I'd say that's your best bet. Although convincing Matix to let you have it will be a task and a half."

You thank the stevedore for his help and head towards Matix's house.

As you make your way to the north of the island, you see a port for a Goblin flyer which can take you to Asperitas.

If you want to head for the flyer, turn to **323**. If you want to continue to Matix's home, turn to **161**.

75

As you get nearer to the waterfall, you spy tracks in the mud. You crouch down. They look like paw prints, and fresh ones at that. You look up beyond the waterfall and see a Goblin flyer moored at the top of the cliffs. You could use it to travel to more of the islands. But is your work on Altos done?

If you decide to investigate the paw prints, turn to **299**. If you decide to investigate the Goblin flyer, turn to **361**.

76

You attempt to track the flying eye from below, on the streets of Asperitas. Unfortunately, it spots you and zooms off. You run after it. *Test Your Stamina*. It you are Successful, turn to **13**. If you are Unsuccessful, turn to **87**.

77

You ask them what they remember about what happened.

"Not much," says the first Officer, who tells you his name is Ferris. "We were all gathered in the Great Hall at Elder Vizigg's request, and then there was this loud *stomping* sound, followed by lots of screaming. I remember something big – really big. Maybe some kind of giant. I think I blacked out. When I came to, there was this enormous explosion and we started falling. Then I . . . er . . . blacked out again."

If you want to ask Ferris what's wrong with the injured Officer (if you haven't already), turn to **356**. If you want to ask if there are any other survivors, turn to **197**. If you have asked him everything you want to, turn to **330**.

78

First one scaly head emerges from the widening pool, then a second. You realize that Boreas has summoned a fearsome Hydra to fight you, and from the surprised then delighted look on the Stormborn's face, you suspect even he wasn't sure what he was summoning.

HYDRA   *SKILL 9*   *STAMINA 13*

If you win, turn to **392**.

79

Holding your nose, you continue into the sewers, following the creature's tracks. Turning a corner, you see the giant insect just about to climb up a small pipe with your Coin Bag in its mandibles. Quickly you whip out your Short Sword and hurl it at the retreating bug.

Test Your Skill. If you are Successful, turn to **383**. If you are Unsuccessful, turn to **275**.

80

Grax gestures to a nearby contraption. "Just put 1 Gold Piece in the slot and place your hovers' storm crystal in the chamber."

When you do so (deduct 1 Gold Piece), there is a loud *whirring* noise and the little storm crystal begins to glow brightly. The tiny tempest inside whirls away happily.

You're now ready to take off and visit Altos or Cumulus.

To fly to Altos, the water island, turn to **164**. To fly to Cumulus, the island of trade, turn to **146**.

81

You lower your sword and tell him that he'd better not cross your path again, or you won't be so merciful.

"Thank you, thank you," he whimpers. "I'll find a way to help you, I promise." He passes you a crumpled note. "See, see! I was telling the truth!" With that, he dashes out of the door.

At the codeword **Galen** to your Adventure Sheet.

You unfold the note. It reads:

Whatever you do, don't go to the Nimbus this morning.

Your friend,

Paxlo

You recognize the name as being that of a Goblin who works on Asperitas, the island of technomancy. You also find an Apple.

(Add the Crumpled Note to the Equipment Box on your Adventure Sheet and the Apple to your Provisions, making a note that it will restore up to 2 *STAMINA* points when eaten.)

You leave the Watchhouse.

If you have not already visited the Great Waterfall, and want to do so now, turn to **328**. If you would prefer to find the nearest flyer so you can get off this island, turn to **361**.

82

When you ask Vizigg what happened to the Nimbus, he looks downcast.

"I called the Sky Watch to the Nimbus in order to expose Krazic's plan, but his weapon was more powerful than I had imagined. He turned it on us all. I had no choice but to overload all the storm crystals in the vicinity. It took down Krazic's creation, yes, but the Nimbus with it."

To ask what befell the Technomancer, if you haven't already, turn to **11**. If you want to ask what Vizigg is doing with the broken storm crystals, and haven't already, turn to **59**. If you want to ask about the ward on the Great Hall, and you haven't already, turn to **338**. If you are done asking him questions, turn to **170**.

83

The door looks too solid to break. Next to the door there is a sequence of carved numbers: 1, 4, 9, 18, 35, - ?

Below are the numbers 0–9 on carved blocks, which you notice have little springs under them. You're guessing that you have to enter the next number in the sequence. Once you have worked out what it should be, turn to that section number.

If you cannot solve the puzzle, then you have no choice but to leave the bell tower and head north-east, back into the maze of workshops and laboratories, turn to **111**.

84

The last of the storm crystal's energy is draining away when Cirrus comes into view. You're relieved to see this green and pleasant isle, which produces much of the magically enhanced fruit, vegetables and grains that feed Pangaria. Inexperienced at guiding the hovers, you make a swift but shaky descent. The lush, verdant turf of Cirrus rushes up to meet you.

Test Your Luck. If you are Lucky, turn to **36**. If you are Unlucky, turn to **151**.

85

You direct the *Barnacle* towards the caves. Fish, coral and other aquatic life forms of every colour imaginable drift around you, busy with their own affairs and seemingly unperturbed by you and your squat little craft. Soon you come to the entrance to the caves.

The cave entrance is wide, and you easily manoeuvre the bathysphere inside. Even in this darker world, there are bright spots of luminescent plant life and eyes watch you from every nook and crevice. You reach a fork in the caves.

If you want to take the left fork, turn to **231**. To take the right fork, turn to **101**.

86

You take your sharpest blade and finish Caleb before whatever is inside him can do the job for you. You drive your weapon into the mass of tentacles beneath his skin and they cease their movement. You're very glad that you never had to see what they belonged to.

Leaving the poor Caleb lying on the floor of the shed, you hurriedly leave, feeling that it is urgent you finish your quest before any more islanders suffer such a horrible fate.

If you have the codeword **Renard** written on your Adventure Sheet, turn to **56**.

If not, where do you want to go now? To head north towards Matix's home, turn to **161**. To head to the east dock and the bathysphere workshop, turn to **74**.

87

You just about manage to keep up with the flying eye, but it takes a lot out of you. (Lose 1 *STAMINA* point.) Turn to **38**.

88

The usual bustling sounds of the market are more muted today. You don't see as many stalls open, and the crowds are decidedly sparser than usual. The explosion on Nimbus has driven many indoors, but the stallholders are hardier and won't run and hide if there's even one person to make money from.

You need to get some tips on what's been happening

around here from the local stallholders, but they won't give up the gossip unless you buy something from them. You browse a nearby stall.

You can buy some bread for 1 Gold Piece (which will restore 2 *STAMINA* points) or an apple pie for 2 Gold Pieces (which will restore 3 *STAMINA* points) or a Healing Potion for 2 Gold Pieces (which will restore 4 *STAMINA* points).

Choose what you want to buy and turn to **227**.

89

You pull down *Winged Menaces: Death from Above*. A beam of light projects from the book on to the ceiling and a magical portal opens. You hear a loud buzzing sound and a Giant Wasp emerges from the portal. The overgrown insect heads straight for you, its stinger at the ready.

GIANT WASP *SKILL 6* *STAMINA 6*

The first time an attack from the Giant Wasp succeeds, it will do the usual amount of damage, but it will also leave its barbed sting impaled in you. This causes a further 2 *STAMINA* points and 1 *SKILL* point of damage.

If you win, turn to **263**.

The peace is interrupted by the sound of screams and clashing met

90

The peace is interrupted by the sound of screams and clashing metal. You follow the noise towards one of the docks. You reach it to find a couple of fishermen in a frantic battle with an enormous crustacean. You fear the energies released from the explosion on Nimbus are responsible. The fishermen aren't faring at all well, and you see them get swept aside by the creature's massive claws before it starts smashing through some nearby boats. It's up to you to stop it now.

GIANT CRAB   *SKILL 8*   *STAMINA 9*

If you win, turn to **199**.

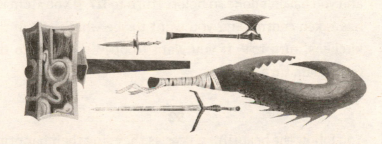

91

You and Silas grab a bed each and sleep for a fitful hour or so. In your dreams you are flying through the Pangarian skies, trying to catch your falling Sky Watch friends. They cry out to you as they tumble through the air. You save one, but more fall away from your grasp.

You grab for a flailing arm, only to realize that it's your own face that you're staring into. You try to hold on, gripping tighter, but it's no good. You watch as your screaming face falls away from you, limbs flailing uselessly, dropping away into nothingness.

It might not be peaceful, but at least it's sleep (add 2 *STAMINA* points to your Adventure Sheet).

You awake to find Silas tugging at your arm. Turn to **395**.

92

You arrive back in the Nimbiferous Chamber.

If you want to venture down the half-flooded hallway, and you haven't done so before, turn to **127**. If you stomach has taken control and you want to see what's left in the kitchens, turn to **9**. If you want to open the door to the Great Hall, turn to **369**.

93

You follow the beautiful voices as they sing their haunting melody out into the storm. Then suddenly, through the wind and the rain, you see them. Beautiful female figures sitting on the rocks ahead – human to the waist, with long colourful fish tails that shine with an iridescent light. The figures are brushing their hair and giving voice to the most beautiful melody you've ever heard. It seems to go right through you, making your skin tingle. Do you want to:

Draw closer to these beautiful figures?   Turn to **157**.

Turn the bathysphere around and head for the stranded boat, if you haven't already?   Turn to **215**.
Dive below the sea?   Turn to **203**.

94

You show Caleb the Ledger page with *Commander Mathias Talliman* written on it and the words *Where is he?* scrawled next to the name.

"Talliman! That's it. That's the one! Hmm, where is he? Someone seems interested in his whereabouts. Wonder why? The last I heard he was recuperating with the Renard family over near the north docks. Not seen them for a while though, so no idea how he's doing."

(Add the codeword **Renard** to your Adventure Sheet.)

Caleb starts coughing even harder, like he's struggling for breath again. He rubs his chest as if it's causing him pain.

If you want to ask more about the *Doombringer*, and you haven't already, turn to **33**. If you want to leave Caleb in peace and continue your journey, turn to **295**.

95

As you dispense the killing blow, the Lightning Serpent sinks back into the mist, which melts away, leaving the bridge swaying in the bright sunshine. At your feet you see Daxa's aeronaut's helmet. You pick it up and put it on, grateful that Goblins have surprisingly large heads for their size. You feel better protected and you notice that there's a crystal visor built into the helmet. You flip the visor down and your vision becomes much sharper. You realize it must be magically enhanced.

Wearing the aeronaut's helmet will permanently add 1 point to your *SKILL* score, even if this takes it beyond its *Initial* level. Also, if you suffer a hit from a weapon in battle, roll one die and on a roll of 5 or 6, you may reduce the damage done by 1 *STAMINA* point. (Add the aeronaut's helmet to your Adventure Sheet.)

With the bridge now open, you can continue to Cirrus. Turn to **232**.

96

You put 1 Gold Piece in the slot of the little machine and place your hovers' storm crystal inside the charging chamber.

There is a loud whirring noise and the little storm crystal begins to glow brightly. The tiny tempest inside starts to whirl again.

You are now ready to take off and visit Cirrus or Cumulus.

If you want to fly to Cirrus, the farming island, turn to **220**. If you want fly to Cumulus, the island of trade, turn to **140**.

97

You drop to the ground and accidentally put your hand on a broken piece of glass (lose 2 *STAMINA* points). You stifle your pain and pull yourself behind cover. Turn to **162**.

98

You tell Vizigg that you believe a Stormborn is involved. Vizigg nods. "That is correct, Officer. Talliman and Krazic enlisted the aid of Boreas the Stormborn, who provided them with crystals for their abomination, and secretly took Talliman back to his homeland. In return the human vowed he would spread news of what would be on offer to whichever warmonger offered the highest price to be split between all three."

To ask what has befallen him, if you haven't already, turn to **11**. If you want to ask him why the Nimbus crashed, and haven't already, turn to **82**. If you want to ask about the ward on the Great Hall, and you haven't already, turn to **338**. If you want to ask what Vizigg is doing with the broken storm crystals, and haven't already, turn to **59**. If you are done asking him questions, turn to **170**.

99

You pass him the Healing Potion. It looks tiny in his hands as he swallows it whole, including the bottle.

(Increase Tideus's *STAMINA* score by 4 points if you have given him a Healing Potion, or by 5 points if you have given him a Greater Healing Potion, and make a note of this on your Adventure Sheet.)

"Much betta! Got anyfin else, hooman?"

If you want to give Tideus a Potion of Might (and haven't already) turn to **114**. If you want to give Tideus a Potion of Power (and haven't already) then turn to **324**. If you've given him everything you can, turn to **129**.

100

You, Tideus and the Goblin War Golem are flagging. The fight is almost over for one of you. Continue the battle until either the Sea Giant or the War Golem is beaten.

If you and Tideus win the battle, turn to **69**. If the War Golem wins the battle, turn to **334**.

101

You glide the bathysphere down the gloomy tunnel to the right. The *Barnacle* floats through narrow tunnels and small caves with ease, aside from a few small scratches to its hull, but there seems little of interest in the murky depths.

You're just about to give up and go back when the tunnel becomes lighter. You can't see what's producing the illumination.

If you want to press on, hoping to find the source of the light, turn to **190**. If you want to turn back and leave the caves, turn to **61**.

102

You knock at the door. Nothing.

You knock again, calling out, "Sky Watch! Open up!"

There's the sound of *muttering* inside and you hear a door slam. Whoever was lurking inside must have left via the back door. You try the front door, but discover it's locked.

If you want to go round to the back door, turn to **209**. If you want to try to force the front door, turn to **72**.

You guide your hovers towards Altos. You've not had a chance to visit it before, during your brief time in the Sky Watch, and as you descend, the sentient clouds which are farmed there – known as Cloudkin – scatter like frightened sheep. Some of them shed a little water as they float speedily away from you.

You drink in the beautiful sight of Altos from above. Lakes, rivers and waterfalls sparkle in the sunshine.

But in your joy at seeing Altos, you fly too close to a Mother Cloudkin, who has several young Cloudkin drifting around her. The young ones flee to their mother in fright and fold themselves into her fluffy, cloudy depths. She angrily lashes out at you with a bolt of lightning which strikes your hovers and sends you tumbling to the ground. (Lose 3 *STAMINA* points.)

If you're still alive, you try to scrape off the worst of the mud. Your hovers aren't badly damaged, but are out of charge, so you will need to find some way of charging them up in order to fly anywhere else. For now, you're on foot.

You look for a place to start your investigation. You see a nearby Cloudkin farm. Perhaps the farmer will be able to help you with supplies and information. Turn to **30**.

The whirling mass lifts you into the air. Higher and higher. Even if you had charge left in your hovers, they wouldn't help you in the midst of this chaotic wind.

You struggle and flail against the invisible force. Then suddenly you're falling. You expect to feel the crush of the cold, hard ground, but instead you're caught in mid-air by ethereal arms.

The figure floats to the ground and places you down safely.

"I'm sorry about that," says the figure. "I had no idea anyone was out here, and the storms can be quite temperamental, especially at the moment."

You're being addressed by a Stormborn – one of the intelligent wind spirits that create and harvest crystals within the storms that rage across the Sea of Tempests. The figure, who you rightly assume to be Methedus, waves his hands through the air like he's conducting an invisible orchestra and the cyclone slows its whirling and glides towards the windmill. It spreads out over the sails and they creak into life.

"How may I help you, Officer?"

You tell Methedus that you're looking into what happened at the Nimbus.

"We Stormborn we very concerned by what happened," he says sadly. "All of us who live and work in Pangaria felt it in every fibre of our beings. That means the amount of elemental energy released must have been immense. Many storm crystals must have been broken.

"Of course, we tried to reach the Nimbus, but although we can pass safely through the storms that surround it, there is a warding spell around the island preventing Stormborn from entering. Someone clearly doesn't want us interfering."

(Write the codeword **Bubble** on your Adventure Sheet.)

If you have the storm crystal shard from Cirrus, turn to **5**. If you do not have the storm crystal shard from Cirrus, turn **205**.

105

You glide down on to the green and pleasant isle of Cirrus, which produces much of the magically enhanced fruit, vegetables and grains that feed Pangaria. You have little experience of this isle, but you're nervous about what the magical energy released by Nimbus may have done to the vegetation. You look around and spot a plume of blue-green smoke in the distance. You also realize that the local Watchhouse is not too far away. That might be worth visiting for supplies.

To investigate the plume of blue-green smoke, turn to **137**. To investigate the local Watchhouse, turn to **49**.

106

The Octopus abruptly releases its hold on the wretch and drops to the ground, leaving the fisherman gasping for breath.

If you want to try to speak to the man, turn to **266**. If you prefer to finish him, while you have the advantage, continue the fight and if you win, turn to **213**.

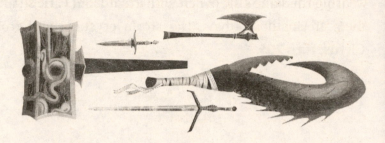

107

You pass him a Healing Potion (remove it from your Adventure Sheet.) He gulps it down.

"Ah, that's the good stuff! Thank you, friend."

He apologizes for not having anything for you in return, and you remember than sometimes a kind deed well received is reward enough. (Gain 2 *LUCK* points.)

If you want to ask them what happened to the Nimbus, turn to **77**. If you want to ask if there are any other survivors, turn to **197**. If you feel as if you have asked them enough questions, turn to **330**.

108

You dispense the last destructive blow. The five digits of the hand shudder and go still. To your surprise, a dead Goblin falls out of it. You notice the creature is wearing a belt with an ornate brass buckle with a letter *P* engraved on it.

There's an anguished cry. Another Goblin rushes up and kneels beside the body. He has tears in his eyes and is wearing the same kind of belt with a matching *P*. He shakes the dead Goblin's body.

"Why did you do it? Why wouldn't you listen to me? I told you it was too dangerous!"

You give the Goblin space to grieve for a moment, and then ask to speak to him. He suddenly throws a handful of powder in your face and you black out.

Lose 2 *STAMINA* points and, if you are still alive, turn to **198**.

109

The rabid Corn Rats lay slain at your feet. You notice two ears of ripe corn have fallen to the ground during the battle. (Add 2 ears of corn to the Provisions Box on your Adventure Sheet; each one will restore 3 *STAMINA* points when eaten.)

To continue to the Watchhouse, turn to **243**.

"Only one of us is getting out of this Watchhouse alive"

You stand up to see a fellow Sky Watch Officer, looking confused and holding a burning log from the fire.

"Who are you?" the man asks. "And how did you get out of the Cita—"

He stops himself. You feel the anger rising within you. Did this Sky Watch Officer know what was going to happen at the Citadel? Before he can react, you pin him against the wall with your sword at his neck, and demand he tells you what he knows.

"Nothing, I swear! I just got a message saying not to go to the meeting at the Nimbus this morning. It didn't say why. When I saw what happened, I decided to hide out here."

You ask him who the message was from. He's hesitant to answer, and although you hate to threaten a fellow member of the Sky Watch, this is no time for secrets. You push the cutting edge of your sword against his throat.

"Easy, easy, you wouldn't kill a fellow Sky Watch Officer, would you?

You relax your grip and lower your sword. The man seizes the opportunity and shoves you back hard. By the time you regain your balance, he has grabbed a sword of his own.

"Only one of us is getting out of this Watchhouse alive. And I'm telling you now, pal, it's gonna be me."

SKY WATCH OFFICER   *SKILL 7*   *STAMINA 7*

If you manage to reduce your opponent's *STAMINA* score to 3 points or fewer, turn to **374** at once.

111

You decide to head toward the maze of workshops and laboratories, even though you're not sure where to start. As you walk through the bustling alleyways, you listen to the gossip to see if you can find a lead. Sure enough, you hear talk about a strange piece of metal which fell on one of the old workshops to the east.

If you want to head off to investigate for yourself, turn to **325**. If you want to head towards where the residents of Asperitas live, if you haven't done so already, turn to **293**.

If you are ready to leave the island and return to Incus, turn to **379**.

112

You move your bathysphere closer to the bubble and see that Methedus is inside it.

"Ah, you're still alive!" he grins. You realize that Matix's amplification device is allowing you to hear him perfectly, even inside the bathysphere.

"I hoped you would be. I came to give you this. I thought it might come in handy."

Methedus waves his hands and creates a small bubble in which floats a Potion of Power. He pushes the little bubble through the walls of his own and floats it across to the *Barnacle*, where you can capture it.

(Add the Potion of Power to your Adventure Sheet. This will increase your Attack Strength by 2 points for the duration of one fight only and restore 3 *STAMINA* points.)

"The Stormborn ward is still active around Nimbus. And until it is lifted, none of us can help the island. It's up to you now, Officer."

With that, Methedus and his bubble float back to the surface. Turn to **3**.

113

You easily manage to summon the strength to pull the last of the debris from Captain Halleck's legs. They are so badly damaged he can hardly walk, so you find him a more comfortable place to rest. Turn to **148**.

114

You throw Tideus the Potion of Might. He gulps it down.

(Increase both Tideus's *SKILL* score and his *STAMINA* score by 2 points, and make a note of these alterations on your Adventure Sheet.)

"Ah yes! Tideus is indeed mighty! Yous gots more?"

If you want to give Tideus a Healing Potion or a Greater Healing Potion (and you haven't already), then turn to **99**. If you want to give Tideus a Potion of Power (and you haven't already), then turn to **324**. If you've given him everything you can, turn to **129**.

115

You give Vizigg the silver goblet. "That will do nicely," he says, taking it from you.

If you have a copper ring, turn to **228**. If you have a black candle, turn to **6** If you want to leave the Under-Library and go in search of these items, turn to **26**. If you have given Vizigg all the requested items, turn to **206**.

116

"Because Pox's got in for me, that's why! Him and his brother, Paxlo!" says Yurik angrily. "Ever since I said I didn't want to join his damn workshop crew and their so-called secret project over at Nimbus. If things sound too good to be true, they usually are!"

If you want to ask about the workshop and the secret

project, turn to **133**. To lie and tell Yurik that you know he was behind it, turn to **372**. If you want to leave, you can head west towards where the residents of Asperitas live, turn to **293**. Or if you want to head north, further into the maze of workshops and laboratories, turn to **111**.

117

You head up on to the rooftops. You get a good view over the marketplace, but there's no sign of the creature. The way ahead looks a little unstable, but you pick up the sound of *chittering* at the edge on your hearing.

Do you want to venture further onwards, return to the street and try the storm drain, or continue onwards without your gold?

To continue over the rooftops, turn to **70**. To return to the street and investigate the storm drain, turn to **171**. To abandon your gold and continue to the far side of the market, turn to **336**.

118

You head for the Renard house Caleb told you about. You can't remember the last time someone from the outside world was brought to Pangaria. You've always thought it was a little unfair that they weren't allowed to return to their homeland. But given that the alternative would be death, then building a new life in Pangaria is hardly the worst thing to have to endure.

You finally reach the Renard house on the edge of the island. It is quiet and there's no answer when you knock at the door. That's unusual; someone should be home at this time of day. You push the door gently and it swings open. You gingerly head inside.

As you enter the house, you call out to the Renard family. There's no answer.

The house is in a complete mess. It looks like a hurricane got trapped inside. Furniture is upended, books and toys lie strewn about, and pictures have been knocked off the walls. It's very strange.

There's a *creaking* above you and the sound of breaking wood.

Test Your Luck. If you are Lucky, turn to **207**. If you are Unlucky, turn to **354**.

119

The Wheelies crash to the floor, rock backwards and forwards for a bit, and then lie still. You wonder why whoever lives here needs Wheelies to guard them.

If you decide to head for the upper floor, turn to **350**. If you want to look around the ground floor, turn to **182**.

120

You press on through the storm, hoping that you will find the Nimbus in the middle of it somewhere. Suddenly you hear singing coming from somewhere outside the bathysphere. It's beautiful. You also spy what looks like a stranded boat bobbing up and down in the waves.

If you want to follow the sound of the singing, turn to **93**. If you want to investigate the stranded boat, turn to **215**. If you want to dive below, turn to **203**.

121

You wait out of sight, until Methedus has gone back into the mill, and then quietly approach. You walk round the outside of the building until you find a small window. Climbing on some flour bags, you look through it and see Methedus, sitting cross-legged whilst floating in the air, and looking like he's in a trance. That's a strange way to make bread.

One of the bags shifts beneath you and you gasp as you fall to the ground (lose 1 *STAMINA* point).

You look up and see Methedus staring down at you from the window.

"You'd better come inside, Officer." Turn to **46**.

122

You pick up the paper the creature dropped. Strangely, it appears to be blank. You take it to the desk to examine it more closely. The desk is littered with scrawl-covered papers, and most of the writing is illegible. Nearby you see a couple of squeezed lemon halves and a small lamp. Do you want to:

Rub the lemon over the paper?   Turn to **253**.

Light the lamp and hold the paper close
to it?   Turn to **218**.

Leave the tower and head north-east, back
to the maze of workshops and laboratories.   Turn to **111**.

123

Checking all the chests, you discover that one of them is unlocked.

If you want to search the unlocked chest, turn to **371**. If you want to leave the Watchhouse, turn to **335**.

124

You never thought you would find yourself lighting a fire in the depths of the ocean.

The fire soon dries you off and you start to feel a little more like yourself. (Regain up to 3 *STAMINA* points.) Once you are dry, you carefully put out the fire and continue with your exploration. Turn to **288**.

125

You pass the Thingie to Matix and she looks delighted. "That's a hell of a Thingie you've found. Well done, Officer!"

If you have a Wotsit or Doobry, and haven't already given the item to Matix, you can do so now, by turning to **375**. If you have now given Matix everything she requested, turn to **187**. If you need to get your hovers charged up again, turn to **396**.

126

You see the bell tower, which Yurik mentioned, in the distance. But you're increasingly feeling like you need to get to a more populous part of the island, rather than keep wandering around out here on your own.

To head to the bell tower, turn to **352**. To head north-east back to the maze of workshops and laboratories, turn to **111**.

127

The water looks murky, but you have no choice but to venture into it. At first it just comes up to your waist, but soon you realize you're going to have to swim for it.

Roll one die. If you roll a 1 or 2, turn to **139**. If you roll a 3 or 4, turn to **310**. If you roll a 5 or 6, turn to **145**.

128

You dive for cover, but don't quite manage to protect yourself completely. A lump of rumble hits you hard on the shoulder. (Lose 2 *STAMINA* points.) Turn to **208**.

The War Golem strides forward

You've prepared Tideus for the battle ahead as well as you can.

"Now dis is a proper fight, hooman!"

And it will be, because although the Goblin War Golem is taller than Tideus, the Sea Giant is broader and built like a green granite cliff.

"Yous not missing out on dis, hooman!" Tideus bellows, picking you up and placing you on his shoulder, like some kind of human parrot. "Yous can get some hits in too!"

"Ha!" shrieks Krazic. "You think that mound of blubber is going to stop me?"

The War Golem strides forward. It is missing one hand but has replaced it with a large piece of masonry, to use as a makeshift club. In the other hand it wields a huge axe.

The fight is on!

GOBLIN WAR GOLEM   *SKILL 11*   *STAMINA 30*

Tideus will have whatever *SKILL* and *STAMINA* you have managed to grant him with your potions, or not, as the case may be. Because you are assisting him in this battle, you may add 2 points when calculating the Sea Giant's Attack Strength, and you may increase any damage he causes by 1 point. However, if Tideus is killed in his battle against the War Golem, you will die too!

If you and Tideus are the first to win two of the first

three Attack Rounds, turn to **222**. If the Goblin War Golem is the first to win two of the first three Attack Rounds, turn to **174**.

130

The spell leaves the chest and the lid sinks down, lifeless once more. Inside you find a flask of fire oil and a piece of paper. You unfold the paper carefully. It looks like a page torn out of a ledger from one of the fishery docks in Incus. A few names are marked on the page, but one name, *Commander Mathias Talliman*, has been circled several times. Scrawled next to it are the words *Where is he?*

You can add the Incus ledger page and the fire oil to the Equipment List on your Adventure Sheet.

(The fire oil can be used once to light a fire, or it can be used against an opponent at the start of a battle, and will automatically cause your enemy 3 *STAMINA* points of damage.)

That last fight really took it out of you, and you realize that you've been held up by a mixture of fear, adrenalin and anger until this point. Now you could do with a little old-fashioned shut-eye.

If you want to take a nap, turn to **184**. If you would rather leave the Watchhouse, turn to **335**.

131

You arrive at the Altos Watchhouse. You try the door but discover it's locked. You press your ear to the wood. As Nemi said, the sound of loud *snoring* can be heard coming from inside. You need to get inside somehow.

If Nemi is with you, turn to **251**. If Nemi is not with you and you want to break the door down, turn to **67**. If you have some corrosive grapes and you want to use them on the door lock, turn to **380**.

132

You head up to the surface to try to find the stranded boat. The storm is still raging and it's disorientating. Suddenly a beautiful melody floats out of the mist towards you. It seems to wrap your whole body in warmth and light. It's the most beautiful thing you've ever heard.

At the same time, you see a glowing light breaking through the mist. It winks on and off.

If you want to follow the sound of the singing, turn to **264**. If you want to investigate the light, turn to **305**. To dive back to the caves if you haven't finished exploring them, turn to **85**. To dive towards the large dim shape, turn to **191**.

133

You ask Yurik about the workshop crew on Nimbus and their secret project.

"No!" says the Goblin, resolutely folding his arms. "I'm not saying another word, and I'm guessing with all your Sky Watch friends having a little swim right now, you don't have time to hang around pestering me! All I'll say is, find Pox and Paxlo. Then you'll get some answers!"

And with that he runs inside the workshop and slams the door. There are some loud *clanking* noises that put you in mind of a sophisticated lock being triggered.

You bang on the door, but there's no answer.

You decide what to do next. You notice a device nearby that charges storm crystals. You remember that there are quite a few of them dotted around Asperitas and for 1 Gold Piece, you can use the device to charge your hovers and return to Matix on Incus, when you need to.

If you want to try and break down the door, turn to **21**. Alternatively you can head west, towards where the residents of Asperitas live (turn to **293**), or head north, deeper into the maze of workshops and laboratories (turn to **111**).

134

Silas gestures to one of the chests. "The lock on this one looks pretty old," he says. "I reckon I can get it open with my pitchfork."

He levers the pitchfork under the lock and lifts it sharply. The lock breaks with a *clank*. He peers inside and begins to poke through its contents with his pitchfork.

"Phew! Someone in here does not like to wash their socks! Hmm, these could be useful."

He passes you a Potion of Might and 1 Gold Piece. (Potion of Might will add 2 points to your Attack Strength for the duration of one battle. Record these in the Equipment and Gold boxes on your Adventure Sheet.)

What's left for you to do?

If you want to check your chest, if you haven't already done so, turn to **217**. If you want to search the unlocked chest, if you haven't already done so, turn to **65**. If you want to leave the Watchhouse, turn to **335**.

135

You ask Yurik what he was talking about when you first met.

"Well, I mean, Nimbus falling of course! It's all anyone's talking about."

He's right about that, but why would he think you suspected him?

If you want to ask him why he thinks you might believe he's involved, turn to **116**. If you want to lie and accuse Yurik of being behind it, turn to **372**.

136

You head back to the bathysphere. Seems like you still have some exploring to do.

Do you want to go to the flooded right-hand passageway off the antechamber, if you haven't done so already (turn to **344**), or do you want to leave the Citadel (turn to **256**)?

137

You make your way across Cirrus towards the blue-green plume of smoke. Worried farmers approach you asking about what happened on Nimbus. All you can tell them is to keep calm, stay indoors and that the Sky Watch is looking into it. You manage to sound more convincing than you feel.

When you reach the edge of the field that is the source of the smoke plume, you realize that it's not smoke at all but a swirling blue-green mist, which is coming from a large storm crystal shard that is half-embedded in the middle of a cabbage field, close to a small shed. It looks like a much bigger version of the one in the hovers nestled on your back, although it's very cracked and clearly badly damaged. It must have landed here after the explosion on the Nimbus.

If you want to charge up your hovers' storm crystal and Silas is with you, turn to **51**.

If you want to charge up your hovers' storm crystal and Silas is not with you, turn to **211**.

If you want to investigate the shed, turn to **376**.

138

You aim for a soft-looking haystack. Unfortunately, you completely miss your target. Your hovers' wings fold up and you are deposited into a nearby rubbish heap, where you hit your head on a piece of broken pot. (Lose 3 *STAMINA* points.)

If Cumulus is your home isle, turn to **57**. If Cumulus is not home isle, turn to **88**.

139

You're a strong swimmer, but when you feel something bite down on your foot, you start floundering and kick out. You feel your boot strike something, which swims away, but the damage is done. Lose 3 *STAMINA* points and then turn to **73**.

140

You decide to visit Cumulus, the island of trade. You check the hovers, make a running jump and take off, the waters of Altos sparkling beneath you.

(If you had Nemi with you, she will stay on Cumulus and you will lose your attack and damage bonuses. Adjust this on your Adventure Sheet.) Turn to **193**.

141

Dav picks up a large purple tuber from a nearby stall and hurls it after the creature. The root vegetable strikes the Cockroach's shell, causing it to stagger briefly, shedding 1 Gold Piece from the bag. (Add this back to the Gold Box on your Adventure Sheet.) Unfortunately, the tuber strike was only enough to slow the creature down briefly. It readjusts its grip on your Coin Bag and skitters off.

If you want to abandon your Coin Bag so that you can continue to the far side of the market, turn to **336**. If you are determined to get it back, turn to **307**.

142

You attempt to track the flying eye from below, on the streets of Asperitas. It suddenly turns towards you. You shrink back into the shadows and hope it hasn't realized you are following it.

Test Your Luck. If you are Lucky, turn to **178**. If you are Unlucky, turn to **245**.

143

You try the lever. Nothing happens. It's been disengaged. You wonder what's happened to whatever was in this room. Turn to **43**.

144

You ask Caleb if he can remember the survivor's name. He thinks for a minute and rubs his neck. You notice there are still nasty red sucker marks where the Octopus gripped him.

"Hmm, military, I think. High up. Sergeant, I think. No, no, Commander. That's it. Commander Tal... Tell... something."

If you have the ledger page from the Cirrus Watchhouse, you can show it to Caleb by turning to **94**.

If not, do you want to ask more about the *Doombringer*, if you haven't done so already (turn to **33**), or continue with your journey (turn to **295**)?

145

You swim strongly through the water. It's almost nice to be engaged in an activity that isn't walking, fighting or being stuck in a metal sphere. You even manage to dive down and pick up a fallen Potion of Might, nestled on a ledge. (Add this to your Adventure Sheet; the Potion of Might will add 2 points to your Attack Strength for the duration of one battle.) Turn to **73**.

146

You decide to visit Cumulus, the island of trade. You check the hovers, make a running jump, and take off, leaving the green fields of Cirrus behind you.

(If you have Silas with you, he will stay on Cirrus and you will lose your attack and damage bonuses. Adjust this on your Adventure Sheet.)

Turn to **193**.

147

You can't take any chances and you prepare to fight the corrupted Canidor.

FLAPPS   SKILL 7   STAMINA 8

If you win, turn to **368**.

After you settle Halleck, you search the kitchen for supplies and find a large cleaver and some pumpkin pie. (Add these to your Adventure Sheet; the pie will restore up to 3 *STAMINA* points when eaten.)

You look up at the hole in the ceiling. You can see various tables and pieces of equipment through it. The room appears to be a workshop. You ask Halleck what was kept in the room above.

"That was Engineer Krazic's private workshop. Most of Pangaria's prototype technomancy was made there."

If you want to climb up to the room above, turn to **212**. If you want to go back to the bathysphere, turn to **152**. If you want to leave via the main door, turn to **378**.

You leave the house and ponder where your investigations should take you next.

You hear a *howl* from a nearby coppice of trees and an ape-like Howl Cat swings down from the branches and lollops towards you, razor-sharp teeth bared and slashing claws ready to tear you apart.

HOWL CAT   *SKILL 8*   *STAMINA 9*

Each time the Howl Cat suffers a hit, it will utter a ferocious battle cry that will deduct 1 point from your

The Great White Squark wants you as its next meal

Attack Strength for the duration of the next Attack Round. However, this also reduces the Howl Cat's *STAMINA* by 1 additional point. If you win, turn to **302**.

150

You direct the *Barnacle* downwards and the waters close over the top of the submersible. Initially your vision is obscured by the churn of the waves, but soon the waters clear and you see the azure ocean stretching out before you.

Unfortunately, this gives you an unusually clear view of the monster heading straight towards you. With the head and upper body of a terrifying shark, and the tentacle-covered lower body of a giant squid, this is the Great White Squark and it wants you as its next meal. Taking a firm hold of the Barnacle's controls, you prepare to battle the sea monster, using the craft's mechanical claws.

GREAT WHITE SQUARK   *SKILL 9   STAMINA 10*

If you win, turn to **385**.

151

As the storm crystal's energy drains from the hovers, you lose control of the wings and crash to the ground, winded, bruised, but alive.

(Roll one die and deduct this many points from your *STAMINA* score.)

When your breath returns, you look out to where Nimbus once was. Now there's nothing but empty space, which crackles with a strange energy. You see a bird fly through it. Tiny forks of lightning target the creature and it explodes in a ball of feather and flames. Whatever took down Nimbus has left danger and death in its wake.

Turn to **321**.

152

You make sure Halleck is comfortable and tell him you're going to continue searching Nimbus. You take the side door out of the kitchen to return to the bathysphere. Once you are inside the vessel again, you return to the antechamber. Turn to **347**.

153

Success! You manage to pull the paper out. It looks like it's fallen out of a diary. The handwriting is smudged and spidery, but you can just make out the following lines.

Pangaria guards its secrets like a dragon squatting on gold! And like such a hoard, their secrets will command a great price on Khul. Krazic and Boreas see the potential here. The Goblin is building something which can be brought to Anghelm in secret. Once Boreas frees me from this place, I will return and tell my commanders of the devastating potential within our grasp. Then we will find the highest bidder!

You recognize Krazic as being the Chief Engineer responsible for maintaining the technomancy which underpins all of Pangaria. Sounds like he has been developing something in secret, but what? And did this cause the fall of the Nimbus?

At first you felt you had some answers, but now you're feeling as if all you've got are more questions.

(Add the codeword **Boreas** to your Adventure Sheet, if you haven't already.)

If you showed the storm crystal shard to Methedus in Cumulus, turn to **345**. If not, there's nothing else to do but press on. To leave and go towards Matix's home, turn to **161**. To leave and head to the east dock and the bathysphere workshop, turn to **74**.

154

You struggle against whatever is restraining you, fervently trying to reach the surface. But it pulls you, down, down, down. You should really heed the warnings about deep, dark waters.

Your adventure is over.

155

You yell in Tideus's ear to "Move!" and he manages to leap out of the way of the falling rubble, meaning you're both unharmed. Tideus even manages to hurl some of the rubble back towards the Goblin War Golem (causing it to lose 3 *STAMINA* points and 1 *SKILL* point).

The Golem launches itself towards the Sea Giant.

Continue the battle between the two colossi. If you and Tideus win two of the next three Attack Rounds, turn to **388**. If the Goblin War Golem wins two of the next three Attack Rounds, turn to **167**.

156

The monstrous harpies lie dead at your feet. You can't help but think that this wasn't a random attack – they were lying in wait for you – but you try not to dwell on this fact too long.

Your eyes and ears are drawn to a gathering of Goblins, who are arguing amongst themselves in a small square.

"We need to get down there!"

"It's too dangerous! We must wait for the storm to pass."

"Then get the Stormborn to go down there!"

"They say there's a ward preventing them from getting close to Nimbus!"

You consider introducing yourself, but you can't get a word in edgeways.

"We need to come up with a plan!"

"Who put you in charge?"

"Well, someone's got to be!"

"But why should it be you?"

"I never said it should be me."

You look around at the squabbling Goblins and know that you stand a better chance of sprouting wings from your ears than they do of agreeing on a plan.

You spy a young Goblin busy cleaning vials and jars outside one of the workshops. You tell the Goblin you're a member of the Sky Watch and a look of horror crosses the Goblin's face. He's so shocked, he drops the vial he's been cleaning, and it smashes on the floor.

"It wasn't me! I didn't have anything to do with it, it was Paxlo and Pox . . . well, probably. I mean, I don't know for sure. But—" he babbles.

This is quite a reaction. You ask the Goblin his name and he tells you that it's Yurik.

To ask Yurik what he's referring to, turn to **135**. To lie and tell Yurik that you know he was behind it, turn to **372**. To help Yurik pick up the pieces of the broken vial, turn to **195**.

157

You move the *Barnacle* closer. There's a sickening *metallic crunch* as your poor bathysphere crashes against the reef. You open the hatch and crawl out, weakly. As you lie dazed on the cold, wet ground, you wonder what rocks are doing in the middle of the ocean anyway.

As the creatures slither over to look at you, their beautiful faces all smiles and laughter, you think you are safe. But their smiles transform into grimaces as their fangs lengthen and their skin turns black. The last thing you remember are their teeth. So many teeth . . .

Your adventure is over.

158

It's only a glancing blow. The contraption emits a high-pitched noise, before flying away up the Watchhouse chimney. You're unharmed but can't shake the feeling that you're being watched.

There's no time to dwell on such things right now, however. There's nothing more to do here, so you leave the Watchhouse. Turn to **335**.

159

You just manage to grab the side of the hole, and with a great deal of scrabbling, you succeed in pulling yourself into the room above. However, you manage to cut yourself in the process (lose 2 *STAMINA* points). Turn to **313**.

160

The log catches you on the side of your head (lose 3 *STAMINA* points and 1 *SKILL* point). Thankfully it's not enough to knock you out, but it makes your head spin.

If Altos is your home isle, turn to **348**. If Altos is not your home isle, turn to **110**.

161

When asked for directions to Matix's house, everyone you speak to tells you to follow the sound of banging and cussing. You soon hear noises that sound like a wheelbarrow being hit with a brick – *thunk, clonk, clang* – and a voice saying, "You son of a rancid hog-mule! You fetid pile of badger excrement! Work, damn you, work!" *Bang! Crash! Thunk!* "Ouch, my thumb!"

At the source of the sound, you find a bathysphere hanging from the rafters of a large workshop, attached to a much smaller house and surrounded by every conceivable tool and mechanical part. The bathysphere is a spherical craft made from reinforced metal, with small porthole-like windows in its sides and a larger one at the front that also doubles as an entry hatch. You notice small storm crystals embedded in the bottom, and large mechanical claws stretching forward from each side. The nameplate on the side of the bathysphere reads *Barnacle*.

You call out Matix's name. Turn to **230**.

162

You get into hiding just as the creature shakes the ash off itself and looks around the room. It's a Winged Gremlin; a particularly nasty little creature. The Gremlin makes straight for Vizigg's desk and starts riffling through the paperwork and sniffing it.

After a minute it seems to have found what it was looking for, and is about to make off with it. But you can't let that happen. You leap out of hiding and throw your weapon at it.

Test Your Skill. If you are Successful, turn to **363**. If you are Unsuccessful, turn to **332**.

163

You attempt to roll away, but the foot gives you a glancing blow on its way down. (Lose 2 *STAMINA* points.)

If you are still alive, turn to **100**.

164

You decide to visit Altos, the water island. You check the hovers, make a running jump, and take off, leaving the green fields of Cirrus behind you.

(If you had Silas with you, he will stay on Cirrus and you will lose your attack and damage bonuses. Adjust this on your Adventure Sheet.) Turn to **103**.

165

You dive for cover and just make it in time. The rubble crashes down beside you, leaving you only lightly dusted. Turn to **208**.

166

(You give Tideus 4 *STAMINA* points' worth of food. Cross this off your Adventure Sheet.) The giant wolfs the food down in one gulp, slaps his hands together and prepares to wrestle you.

TIDEUS   *SKILL 9*   *STAMINA 18*

As Tideus is a little more satisfied, he will give up when you reduce his *STAMINA* score to 10 *STAMINA* points or fewer. When this happens, turn to **267** at once.

167

Krazic shrieks with delight, sensing that victory is close at hand, and swings both the War Golem's weapons, knocking you and Tideus to the ground. You roll off the Sea Giant's shoulder and Krazic urges the mechanical monstrosity forward, intent on crushing you underfoot.

Test Your Skill. If you are Successful, turn to **382**. If you are Unsuccessful, turn to **163**.

The branches are covered with tiny, snapping dragon heads

168

You cautiously follow the sound of the yelling to an orchard. There you find an elderly woman grasping a spade and fending off a marauding fruit tree which has gained both life and an aggressive streak. Instead of the beautiful spiky red fruit that the tree normally bears, the branches are covered with tiny, snapping dragon heads.

One of the heads lunges at the woman and she smacks it with her shovel. The head looks dazed for a moment, and then turns a stream of fire on her. She uses her shovel as a shield, but the metal melts away. She's out of defences.

She drops the melted shovel, rolls up her sleeves and readies her fists. If she's going to go out, she'll go out swinging. But then she spots you.

"Give us a hand, would you, Officer?"

You cannot leave the old woman to fend for herself against the plant, and so you engage the Dragon Fruit Tree in battle yourself.

MARAUDING DRAGON
FRUIT TREE   *SKILL 8*   *STAMINA 9*

If you win, turn to **303**.

You give him 1 Gold Piece and apologize for frightening him.

"Most appreciated, Officer. Look, what I said earlier about not having anything to do with Nimbus falling... I didn't, but I think I know who did. Goblin by the name of Pox or could be his brother, Paxlo. Several months back they started putting together a team to go work in Krazic's workshop on Nimbus."

The young Goblin seems to want to unburden his soul, so you let him talk.

"A plum job! Double wages. But I smelled something off about it. If we took the job, we weren't allowed to tell anyone what we were working on and we had to sleep in the workshop! I like my bed too much to give that up, so I said no. They didn't like that. I've not seen them round here since the Nimbus went down.

"Look, wherever Pox and Paxlo go, trouble follows, that's all I'm saying. Anything else I can help you with? But be quick about it!"

If you have the codeword **Hazi** on your Adventure Sheet, turn to **257**.

If not, and you want to leave, you can head west towards where the residents of Asperitas live (turn to **293**), or north, further into the maze of workshops and laboratories (turn to **111**).

You've heard enough.

"Oh, by the way, what happened to Samuel?" says Vizigg, looking concerned.

Who's Samuel?

"Giant Scorpion. You can't miss him. On guard outside the . . . oh. Ah, never mind. I'm sure he died well."

You quickly ask Vizigg how you can help.

"You are a brave soul to risk your life like this, but this is my mess. It's up to me to repair it."

You tell Vizigg that you didn't come down here to sit around and twiddle your thumbs while the place fills up with water and the air runs out.

"Hmm, well, you are in better condition than me, that's for sure, and perhaps there are places you can get to that I cannot. Very well. To finish the ritual, I need a copper ring, a silver goblet and a black candle.

"Here," he says, tossing you a greater healing potion. "This will help you more than it'll help me." (The potion will restore up to 5 *STAMINA* points.)

If you have a copper ring, turn to **228**. If you have a silver goblet, turn to **115**. If you have a black candle, turn to **6**. If you want to leave the Under-Library and go in search of these items, turn to **26**.

171

You squeeze your way into the storm drain and drop down into the sewer. The smells down here are horrible compared to those in the market above, and make your eyes water. (Lose 1 *STAMINA* point, as the stench starts to make you feel nauseous.) You study the ground and see small tracks in what you hope is only mud.

If you want to follow the tracks, turn to **79**. If you would rather leave the sewer and return to the street, turn to **241**.

172

Hundreds of little fish immediately pop out of their rocky homes and descend on the corpse of the Electric Eel, stripping the flesh from its bones at lightning speed. You hate to think what they might have done to you had you lost the battle. You notice that they leave a strange bulbous object in their wake. It's the eel's Conductive Gland, cackling with elemental energy.

Taking a chance, you skewer it on to the end of one of the *Barnacle*'s pincers. It glints on the end of the weapon.

(The pincer weapon will now cause 3 *STAMINA* points

of damage with each successful hit, rather than the usual 2. Record this on your Adventure Sheet.)

Suddenly you feel more vibrations. The fish go into hiding as the cave roof begins to disintegrate around you, boulders bouncing off the bathysphere's roof with watery *clonks*.

Test Your Skill. If you are Successful, turn to **316**. If you are Unsuccessful, turn to **362**.

173

You attempt to deflect the darts with your cloak. However, one of them grazes your hand. It is coated with poison, but thankfully not too much of it enters your bloodstream; just enough to make your hand go numb. (Lose 2 *STAMINA* points and 1 *SKILL* point.)

You continue upwards cautiously until you reach a locked door. Turn to **83**.

174

Krazic yells in triumph! You wonder what you can do to swing the battle in your favour.

If you have the trident, you can pass it to Tideus to use; turn to **16**. If you have some fire oil, you can throw it at the Goblin War Golem; turn to **318**. If you have the Giant Crab pincer, you can hurl it at the Goblin War Golem; turn to **39**. If you don't have any of these objects, turn to **326**.

175

There's a ululating cry and two scaly-skinned Kokomokoa emerge from the pool, nets and bamboo spears at the ready. From the confused look on Boreas's face, he was clearly hoping for something a bit more threatening. However, you must fight the amphibious humanoids at the same time.

	SKILL	STAMINA
First KOKOMOKOA	5	5
Second KOKOMOKOA	5	5

The first time a Kokomokoa hits you successfully, the creature will snare you with its a net; do not deduct any *STAMINA* points, but you must reduce your Attack Strength by 2 points from you for the duration of the battle.

If you win, turn to **392**.

176

The contraption emits a high-pitched noise and sends a small fireball towards you.

Test Your Skill. If you are Successful, turn to **202**. If you are Unsuccessful, turn to **58**.

177

"You look like death warmed up, my friend," Silas remarks at your dishevelled appearance. You realize that you've been held up by a mixture of fear, adrenalin and anger until this point. Now you could do with a little old-fashioned shut-eye.

If you want to take a nap, turn to **91**.

Alternatively, choosing something you've not already tried, do you want to search your chest (turn to **217**), see what Silas has found (turn to **134**), or leave the Watchhouse (turn to **335**)?

178

It turns back and flitters on its way. It hasn't seen you. You continue your stealthy pursuit. Turn to **38**.

179

The light dims and the Wraithfish sinks to the bottom of the passageway. You urge the *Barnacle* onwards.

You enter a half-submerged cave, with a rocky ledge on which something has been hoarding various bits of detritus harvested from the sea. There are lots of metallic bits and pieces strewn around the cave. You feel slightly guilty about the fact that the Wraithfish was probably just protecting its shiny things, but they're your shiny things now.

Exiting the bathysphere, you root around amongst the junk to see if you can find anything of value. You find a strange brass rod, which looks like it might have come from an Incus fishing boat, and a silver goblet. (Add both these items to your Equipment List.)

If you have the codeword **Rescue** written on your Adventure Sheet, you can turn to **132**.

If not, and you want to leave the passage and take the left fork in the caves, if you haven't explored that way already, turn to **231**. To leave the caves and head for the large dim shape, turn to **191**.

180

You return to Daxa.

If you want her to charge your flyers for free and fly to Altos, turn to **342**. If you want her to charge your flyers for free and fly to Cirrus, turn to **320**. If you want to take the sky bridge to Cirrus and see if you can find Daxa's aeronaut's helmet, turn to **327**.

181

The Giant Toad disintegrates into a gelatinous heap. You notice some of the goo sticking to a nearby leaf. It has incredible sticking powers. You wrap the leaf around the sticky substance and carefully tuck it away. (Add the sticky toad goop to your Equipment List on your Adventure Sheet.)

You continue towards the Altos Watchhouse. Turn to **131**.

182

Stepping carefully around the Wheelie corpses, you investigate the ground floor. It's so untidy and full of hoarded objects of all kinds, it's hard to tell what might be useful to your investigation and what is just rubbish. You do find a couple of wooden goblets inscribed with "Paxlo" and "Pox".

If you haven't explored the upper floor and want to, turn to **350**. If you want to leave, turn to **149**.

183

You cut open the creature's stomach with your sword. You know that crocodiles have a reputation for eating any old thing they find. You hold your nose as you search the stomach contents and find a Potion of Might and a copper ring. (Add these to your Adventure Sheet. The Potion of Might will add 2 points to your Attack Strength for the duration of one battle.)

If you want to return to Nimbiferous Chamber, turn to **194**. If you want to return to Vizigg, turn to **52**. If you decide to go back to the bathysphere, turn to **136**.

You sleep for a fitful hour or so. In your dreams you are flying through the skies above Pangaria, trying to catch your falling Sky Watch friends. They cry out to you as they tumble through the air. You save one, but more plummet away from your grasp.

You grab for a flailing arm, only to realize that it's your own face that you see staring back at you. You try to hold on, gripping tighter, but it's no good. You watch as your screaming face falls away from you, your limbs flailing uselessly, as your doppelgänger drops away into nothingness.

The sleep isn't peaceful, but it is at least restful (regain 2 *STAMINA* points).

You awake to a strange *buzzing* sound on the edge of hearing, like the rapid flapping of tiny wings.

You peer into the gloom, and in the corner of the barracks you see something that looks like a metal eye. It is about the size of a grapefruit and instead of an iris, you realize that the metal contraption has a large lens. It is held up by small wings, reminiscent of your hovers.

The metal eye zips around, blinking at you. It's very unnerving. You throw your boot at it.

Roll one die. If you roll a 1 or 2, turn to **176**. If you roll a 3 or 4, turn to **158**. If you roll a 5 or 6, turn to **249**.

185

You reassure Hazi that you will check in on Vizigg on Asperitas, and the Goblin thanks you. He reaches into his robe and passes you a couple of items: a piece of dried cuttlefish and an ornate dagger.

(The dried cuttlefish will restore up to 2 *STAMINA* points when eaten, and the ornate dagger will add 1 point to your Attack Strength, if used in battle. Add these items to your Adventure Sheet.)

You notice a sign pointing the way to the local Goblin flyer.

If you want to go to the mill, and haven't done so already, turn to **261**. If you want to go to the flyer and find a way to the other islands, turn to **27**.

186

You engage the bathysphere's controls and decide whether to explore the surface, or dive beneath it.

If you want to dive, turn to **150**. If you want to explore the surface, turn to **312**.

187

"OK, I think I can get her shipshape in a few hours, Officer. Why don't you take a kip in the back there? You're going to need your strength."

You head to the back of the workshop and see a pile of blankets. You're uncertain how clean they are, but you're exhausted, and they do look cosy.

You drift off to sleep, lulled by the sound of *thunks*, *clangs* and the occasional *ouch!*

A few hours later, Matix shakes you awake. "The *Barnacle*'s ready to go. Hope you are too!"

You're not sure that you are, but you follow Matix to the bathysphere, which has been moved to the nearby dock. (Restore up to 2 *STAMINA* points.)

On the way she explains the *Barnacle*'s controls to you. She also tells you how to engage the *Barnacle*'s weapons, which come in the form of large, pincer-like arms, in case you encounter any dangers. There is also a large suction system on one of the pincers for picking up interesting finds you may unearth and bringing them inside the bathysphere.

Matix also tells you she has fitted the *Barnacle* with a special gadget that conducts and amplifies sound, which will allow you to hear better underwater, even from inside the bathysphere.

Upon reaching the *Barnacle*, you climb into the small, one-person cabin, and store your weapons and backpack inside.

"Right! The *Barnacle*'s storm crystals will allow you to float down to the water. You won't find she's as manoeuvrable as your hovers in the air, but once she's in the water, she's a dream! It's all up to you now, Officer. Pangaria's counting on you!"

Matix shuts the lid of the bathysphere and you begin your descent to Nimbus. Turn to **54**.

You walk in on your commanding Officer throwing up into his own helmet. It's quite the sight. You've entered the Citadel kitchens by a side door and can see Captain Halleck pinned under some debris, near a cupboard, not far from the main kitchen entrance. He is surrounded by food remains. He looks at you with bleary eyes.

"You! Wait. . . I don't remember you being at the Citadel. I sent you back for my hovers. How did you get here?" You explain everything that has happened since you parted company, as succinctly as you can.

"By Zephyrus's hurricane heart, you've had quite an adventure! You've done the Sky Watch proud. Er, you couldn't help me with this, could you? It was quite painful to start with, but now I can't really feel my legs any more." He points at the debris pinning him down.

"After Nimbus crashed, I found myself in here. I thought I'd get a bite to eat before searching for survivors, but part of the roof fell in on me."

He points to the ceiling above. There's a big hole in it.

You need to move the debris off Halleck.

Test Your Stamina. If you are Successful, turn to **113**. If you are Unsuccessful, turn to **386**.

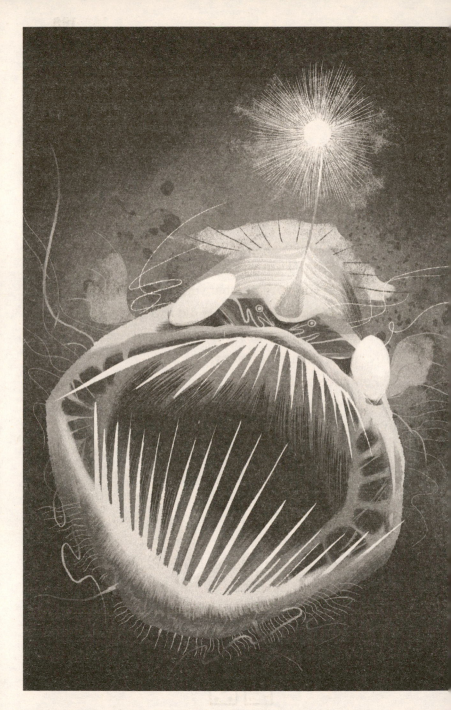

An abyssal horror with a mouth full of needle-sharp teeth

189

You deflect the fireball away from your companion with the blade of your short sword. It crashes harmlessly into the fireplace. The eyeball flies away up the chimney.

You're unharmed but can't shake the feeling that you're being watched. However, there's no time to dwell on such things right now – you need to get moving.

(Write the codeword **Eye-Spy** on your Adventure Sheet.)

Choosing something you've not already tried, will you:

Search your chest? Turn to **217**.

See what Silas found earlier? Turn to **134**.

Leave the Watchhouse? Turn to **335**.

190

The passage becomes narrower, and it's only when the light gets brighter that you realize it's coming from behind you. Right behind you.

This thought is punctuated by a *screeching* sound as something scrapes against the *Barnacle*'s metal hull, and the craft spins forwards, out of control, tumbling you around. (Deduct 2 *STAMINA* points from the *Barnacle*, but also deduct 2 points from your personal *STAMINA* score.)

Once the *Barnacle* is righted again, you speed forward into a larger cave that is only partly submerged. You turn the bathysphere round and face what's behind you.

It is an enormous Wraithfish, an abyssal horror with a

mouth full of needle-sharp teeth and an appendage, like a fishing rod, coming from atop its head, which emits a blinding light. There's no getting around it, you're going to have to fight.

WRAITHFISH   *SKILL 9*   *STAMINA 12*

When you have reduced the Wraithfish's *STAMINA* score to 6 points or fewer, it will knock the *Barnacle* up on to a ledge. The *Barnacle* won't have the manoeuvrability it does in the water, and you will have to reduce its *SKILL* score by 2 points until you can get it back in the water again. If you win, turn to **14**.

191

You direct the *Barnacle* towards the dim shape in the distance. As you get closer the shape gets bigger, and you can make out a familiar fortification. To your horror you realize that you're looking at the Nimbus Citadel. It looks so strange to see it underwater with fish gliding through its gardens. You hope that maybe there are people still alive down there, maybe trapped inside, in no doubt rapidly diminishing air pockets.

A strange object catches your eye. You move closer and realize it's a large air bubble with a figure inside, which barely seems credible.

If you have the codeword **Bubble** on your Adventure

Sheet, you can turn to **112**. If you want to investigate the bubble, and don't have the codeword, turn to **37**. If you want to ignore the bubble entirely and get closer to Nimbus, turn to **3**.

192

Unfortunately, you weaken before the War Golem does and are struck by its axe. (Lose 3 *STAMINA* points.) If you are still alive, turn to **100**.

193

You don't see Cumulus at first, you smell it. The scents drift up to you from the numerous stalls and vendors who trade their wares in the large markets that dominate the island. The soft spicy smells of gingerbread biscuits and cinnamon milk pudding mingle with the pungent aroma of stink fruit and sizzling fish steaks.

A *humming* jolts you from your musings, and the wings begin to shudder. You tense your shoulders and move your upper body as you try to glide yourself down towards a safe and soft landing before the hovers' storm crystal runs out of energy.

Test Your Skill. If you are Successful, turn to **12**. If you are Unsuccessful, turn to **138**.

194

You arrive back in the Nimbiferous Chamber. Will you:

Try the Great Hall door?	Turn to **301**.
Go back to the half-flooded area near the library?	Turn to **236**.
Go to the bathysphere?	Turn to **136**.
Go to the kitchens, if you haven't already?	Turn to **9**.
Return to Vizigg?	Turn to **52**.

195

You help Yurik pick up the broken pieces of the vial. He looks relieved.

"Thank you, Officer. I'm so clumsy. That's the third I've broken today," the Goblin says worriedly. "They're going to start taking it out of my wages if I'm not careful. I've just been so jittery lately."

To ask him what's got him on edge, turn to **4**. To give him 1 Gold Piece to help pay for the damage, turn to **169**.

As you descend towards Altos, the sentient clouds which are farmed there and known as Cloudkin scatter like frightened sheep, some of them shedding a little water as they float speedily away from you. You drink in the beautiful sight of Altos from above. Lakes, rivers and waterfalls sparkle in the sunshine. Despite the horror of what you've witnessed, it gladdens your heart just a little to see your home isle.

But in your joy at seeing Altos, you fly too close to a Mother Cloudkin, who has several young Cloudkin drifting around her. The young ones flee to their mother in fright and fold themselves into her fluffy, cloudy depths. She angrily lashes out at you with a bolt of lightning, which strikes your hovers and sends you tumbling to the ground.

Luckily you land in the mud, dirty and damp, but still alive. (Lose 5 *STAMINA* points.)

You scrape off the worst of the mud and stare across to where Nimbus used to be. Now there's nothing but air and dust, which crackles with a strange energy. Whatever brought the island down must've been incredibly powerful. Sadness gives way to a new resolve. You're going to find out what happened to Nimbus before the rest of Pangaria starts to fall from the sky.

Your hovers aren't badly damaged, but they are out of charge, so you will need to find some way of charging them up in order to fly anywhere else. That means that for now, you're on foot. On the bright side, you've managed to keep hold of Halleck's Coin Bag. You're pretty sure that he won't mind you using it in the line of duty. (Add 10 Gold Pieces to your Adventure Sheet.)

You check your waist. Your trusty short sword is still there. (You can add this to the Weapons Box on your Adventure Sheet.)

You look around for a place to start your investigation. There's a Cloudkin farm nearby. They might be able to help you with supplies and information. Turn to **30**.

197

"I've heard other voices, calling out, crying. But lots of the tunnels are flooded so it's hard to reach anyone. There must be air pockets all over this place. Can't get back into the Great Hall neither. Door must be warded."

If you want to ask what happened to the Nimbus, turn to **77**. If you want to ask what's wrong with the injured Officer, turn to **356**. If you've asked the pair everything you want to, turn to **330**.

198

By the time you come round, both the Goblins have vanished.

You inspect the Giant Metal Hand, which is now thankfully inert. There's an interesting-looking part dangling off the side of it. You give it a tug, and it comes away in your hand. You're no expert, but you think that this might well be a Thingie. (Add the Thingie to your Adventure Sheet.)

You decide what to do next.

You can head to the west towards where the residents of Asperitas live, if you haven't explored that area already (turn to **293**), or you can go to the nearest storm crystal charging station. If you decide to do this, make a note of this section number, as you will be able to return directly to this location if you decide to revisit Asperitas, and turn to **379**.

199

When you finally dispatch the corrupted crustacean, the fishermen come out of hiding, looking extremely relieved.

"Unbelievable," says one of them, shaking his head in amazement. "One moment I'm walking through the fresh catches shed, and the next thing I know, I'm fighting for my life!"

"Still, this'll feed a few families for weeks," says another, examining the corpse.

One of the fishermen gets a large shell-saw and starts

to use it on one of the monster's large claws. He uses a few more implements on it and finally hands you the pincer and some of the crab meat.

The crab pincer smells a bit fishy, but it can be used like a club. (If you use the pincer in battle, you must reduce your Attack Strength by 1 point, but you may increase the damage you cause by 1 point. The crab meat will restore 3 *STAMINA* when eaten. Make a note of this on your Adventure Sheet.)

You ask the fishermen if they know what caused the Nimbus to fall. Turn to **60**.

200

You hand over the item. (Cross it off your Adventure Sheet.) Grax studies it, trying to gauge whether it might help him fix his beloved flyer.

"Yes! Yes! I think that should do the trick. Now all I need is something to glue it down with. You got anything?"

If you have some toad goop or healing honey, turn to **340**. If not, you will have to charge up your hovers – turn to **80**.

201

You yell in Tideus's ear to "Move!" and he manages to leap out of the way of the falling rubble, but you are knocked off his shoulder in the process. (Lose 3 *STAMINA* points and 1 *SKILL* point.)

The Golem launches itself towards the Sea Giant.

Continue the battle between the two colossi. If you and Tideus win two of the next three Attack Rounds, turn to **388**. If the Goblin War Golem wins two of the next three Attack Rounds, turn to **167**.

202

You deftly deflect the fireball with the blade of your Short Sword. It crashes harmlessly into the fireplace, while the eyeball flies away up the chimney.

You're unharmed but can't shake the feeling that you're being watched. However, there's no time to dwell on such things right now. There's nothing more to do here, so you leave the Watchhouse. Turn to **335**.

203

The waters close over you. Initially your vision is obscured by the churn of the waves, but soon the waters clear and you see the azure ocean stretching out before you.

You survey the depths. There's a large, dim shape in the distance. It could be a rock formation, or it could be the sunken Nimbus – you're not sure which.

There are also some interesting-looking caves below you which might be worth investigating too.

If you want to head towards the caves, turn to **85**. If you want to continue towards the dim shape in the distance, turn to **191**.

204

You splash the potion over the overgrown amphibian. Thankfully, the Giant Toad blinks and yawns, then slowly slides back into the swamp it came from.

Cross the Calming Potion off your Adventure Sheet and turn to **131**.

205

Before you go, Methedus passes you a small crystal. It looks like a blank version of the one you have in your hovers.

"You might need this. You seem like the type that gets themselves into trouble. There are a lot of nasty energies around and this will withdraw them from an infected creature, just as long as it's not too far gone. Once an animal's been taken over entirely, the crystal won't work. One use only, I'm afraid." (Add Methedus's shard to your Adventure Sheet and 1 point to your *LUCK* score.)

If you want to look for Hazi on the other side of the market, and haven't done so already, turn to **351**. If you want to find the local Goblin flyer and head for one of the other islands, turn to **27**.

206

You have found everything that Vizigg asked for (regain 1 *LUCK* point), but the old Goblin is getting weaker by the minute. He shuffles round the room, placing the items around the edge of the ritual circle. Nothing happens. He scratches his head. "There's something missing ... now what is it? Damn, it's a storm crystal. Needs to be intact, though. And of course, I destroyed all the ones in the vicinity. Stupid, stupid, stupid!"

To give Vizigg your hovers, turn to **63**. If you would rather leave the library and go exploring, turn to **26**.

207

You manage to jump out of the way as part of the ceiling comes down on the spot where you were just standing.

You also start to notice strange marks on the walls of the house, like ridges or large scratches. Something very strange has happened to the Renard home.

If you have the storm crystal shard from Cirrus, turn to **235**. If you do not have the shard, turn to **279**.

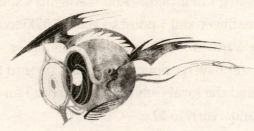

208

Boreas floats in mid-air whilst the storm whirls around him.

"Thank you for freeing our creation and for restoring the Nimbus, Officer," says Boreas smugly. "When you turned up, poking around, I thought you were merely a nuisance I would have to dispatch, or that you would simply die alongside your pathetic Sky Watch friends. But you have proved to be most useful.

"Once we reach Pangaria, Krazic and I will subdue the rest of the islands and continue with our plans. There is great wealth and power to be had out there in the world and it's time to take full advantage of it!"

You tell him that it's over; that the golem is merely a prison for traitorous Goblins now.

"We'll see about that," he sneers.

He begins chanting and a pool of water appears on the floor and from it clambers . . .

Roll one die. If you roll a 1 or 2, turn to **78**. If you roll a 3 or 4, turn to **175**. If you roll a 5 or 6, turn to **391**.

209

You run round to the back door to find it swinging open; someone obviously left in a hurry. An open door is practically as good as an invitation, so you enter the house.

Inside, there are papers strewn about and a coat stand has been knocked over. You're about to head deeper into the house when you hear the noise of something *clattering* down the rickety wooden stairs. This is accompanied by *high-pitched laughter*.

Suddenly you see two disc-like creatures, each with four hands sprouting from their sides. They are holding little knives and are cartwheeling towards you with murder in their eyes.

	SKILL	STAMINA
First WHEELIE	6	6
Second WHEELIE	6	6

If you win tun to **119**.

There's a small robed figure standing at the centre of the circle

210

There's a strange green light emanating from the area ahead. You can hear indistinct muttering and see a large shadow on the wall. You grab a flickering torch from the wall with one hand, keeping your weapon drawn in the other.

You enter the room ahead and can see four large storm crystals at the four compass points of a circle, which are covered in arcane runes, and other miscellaneous objects. You hold up the torch and see that all the storm crystals are broken. There's a small robed figure standing at the centre of the circle. It turns and raises its hand towards you. A strange device on its wrist shoots out a net, which closes around you tightly. You're not going anywhere.

Your attacker shuffles closer and you realize it's Vizigg, the Goblin Elder Technomancer. He looks in a bad way, and there's blood all over his robe.

He peers at you. "Where did you come from?"

You tell him that you came from the surface and you're here to bring those who caused the crash to justice.

He begins to laugh. Turn to **272**.

211

You press your storm crystal to the large shard. A force of energy knocks you back. You hit your head against a piece of rock. (Lose 4 *STAMINA* points and 1 *SKILL* point.) It seems the crystal is too volatile to charge from.

Picking yourself up, you break off a small piece of the

shard near one of the cracks. Strangely, the damage seems to be on the inside of the crystal. You can see worn grooves and cracks on the inside and a strange black residue on the outside. (Record the storm crystal shard on your Adventure Sheet.)

Perhaps you can find someone who'll be able to tell you where the crystal came from and what broke it. Maybe then you'll be able to find out what happened on Nimbus.

If you want to head to the north of Cirrus, in search of a way off the island, turn to **255**. If you want to investigate the shed, turn to **376**. If you want to visit the Watchhouse, turn to **49**.

212

You climb as high as you can in the kitchen and attempt a jump to the hole in the ceiling.

Test Your Skill. If you are Successful, turn to **360**. If you are Unsuccessful, turn to **159**.

213

The poor infected fisherman is dead at your feet. You tell yourself that death by your blade was better than whatever that creature was doing to him. You check his pockets and find 2 Gold Pieces. (Record these on your Adventure Sheet.)

To head north towards Matix's home, turn to **161**. To head to the east dock and the bathysphere workshop, turn to **74**.

214

You're increasingly feeling like you need to get to a more populous part of the island, rather than keep wandering around out here on your own.

You decide to head north-east back to the maze of workshops and laboratories. Turn to **111**.

215

You get closer to the half-wrecked boat and realize it's one of the fishing vessels from Incus. You can see someone sitting in it. You suspect it's an Incus fisherman. You call out, but the man doesn't respond. Is he dead? You draw the bathysphere closer. You can now see by the rise and fall of his chest that he is breathing. You call out again louder.

"Eh?" says the fisherman, removing a tuft of wool from each ear. "Did you say something?"

You ask him why his ears were plugged, and he tells you that there's a group of merfolk nearby. "If you hear too much of their singing, it'll lure you on to the rocks and they'll tear the flesh from your bones."

You ask why he's not taken his boat back to Incus.

"The brass conductor fell off the roof when the Nimbus

crashed down. Can't activate the storm crystals without it," he explains. "Last I saw, it was grabbed by some huge fish with a big old light on its head. It swam off with it!"

You ask if there's anything you can do to help.

"Well, if you can get it back, that would be a good start!"

(Make a note of the codeword **Rescue** on your Adventure Sheet.)

If you agree to help and take the *Barnacle* down, in search of the conductor rod, turn to **22**. If you refuse politely, saying that your priority has to be finding the Nimbus, turn to **349**.

216

Vizigg smiles at you weakly. "That was a kind act, Officer."

You place him down gently, but he drops to the floor. You try to hold him up, but his body seems to have grown heavier with the weight of inevitability.

"We did it," he says weakly. "I'm fading fast, my friend. The rest is up to you now. When I die, the ward around the Great Hall will be broken. You must deal with whatever is left in there. Its existence is too dangerous for it to be allowed to continue; for Pangaria and the world outside. Do you understand me?"

You nod and say you'll do whatever it takes to keep Pangaria safe.

He grasps your collar. "You need to . . . know . . . the . . . Stormborn . . . Boreas. He was there . . . he's dangerous . . .

mad . . . but not as dangerous as . . ."

His voice falters and his eyes go glassy. You feel the old Goblin's small body go limp in your arms. He's gone on to the next world.

There's a loud *thrumming* noise, which you realize must be the sound of the ward around the Great Hall breaking. There's nothing for it but to venture forth and face whatever's in there.

You approach the Great Hall door, half expecting it to be flung open by some terrible monster. Instead everything is eerily quiet.

The Nimbus shakes as it slowly travels upwards towards the surface of the ocean.

Taking a torch from the wall nearby, you enter the Great Hall. Turn to **224**.

217

You search through your meagre possessions and find 2 dried fish, a Healing Potion and 2 Gold Pieces.

(Add the dried fish, Healing Potion and Gold Pieces to your Adventure Sheet. The dried fish will restore up to 2 *STAMINA* points each when eaten and the Healing Potion will restore up to 4 *STAMINA* points when drunk.)

If you want to open the unlocked chest, turn to **65**. If you want to see what Silas has found, turn to **134**. If you want to leave the Watchhouse, turn to **335**.

218

You light the lamp and hold the paper up to the heat. After a while writing begins to appear.

Vizigg,

Krazic is mad. I know that now. Pox doesn't believe me. He is committed to the cause. Krazic must be stopped. It's the only way to save my brother. Please find a way.

Paxlo

Whatever was going on with Paxlo and Pox, a rift seems to have developed between the brothers.

You leave the tower and head north-east back into the maze of workshops and laboratories. Turn to **111**.

219

You use your sword to cut open the creature's stomach. You know such reptiles have a reputation for eating any old thing they find. You hold your nose and search through the stomach contents, finding a Potion of Might and a copper ring. (Add these to your Adventure Sheet. The Potion of Might will add 2 points to your Attack Strength for the duration of one battle.)

You return to the water and heave open the library door. Turn to **18**.

220

You decide to visit Cirrus, the farming isle. You check the hovers, make a running jump and take off, the waters of

Altos sparkling beneath you.

(If you had Nemi with you, she will stay on Altos and you will lose your attack and damage bonuses. Adjust this on your Adventure Sheet.) Turn to **105**.

221

You ask Yurik about Pox and Paxlo.

"Well, if you don't know who they are, then I know you're lying. They've not been seen around here for days. And they're the only ones who'd say such a thing about me. Apart from you, of course. Damn Sky Watch! Hope the lot of you drown!"

And with that he runs inside the workshop and slams the door. (Lose 1 *LUCK* point.)

You bang on the door, but there's no answer.

You decide what to do next. You notice a device nearby that charges up storm crystals. You remember that there are quite a few of them dotted around Asperitas and for 1 Gold Piece, you can use them to charge your hovers and return to Matix on Incus, when you need to.

If you want to try to break down the door bodily, turn to **21**. If not, do you want to head west, towards where the residents of Asperitas live (turn to **293**), or head north, deeper into the maze of workshops and laboratories (turn to **111**)?

222

Krazic is enraged by your success. The Goblin War Golem smashes its stone club into the wall, bringing wood and masonry down on top of you.

Test Your Skill. If you are Successful, turn to **155**. If you are Unsuccessful, turn to **201**.

223

The vines sink to the floor, where they vibrate gently. You tiptoe over them and head out of the Watchhouse. You're just wondering if you should go to the north of Cirrus and locate a flyer to take you onwards to the other islands, when you hear an indistinct yelling in the distance.

If you want to follow the sound of the yelling, turn to **168**. If you want to investigate the plume of blue-green smoke, turn to **137**. If you want to head north, turn to **255**.

224

The first thing you notice in the Great Hall is that there is rubble everywhere. Half the ceiling has collapsed and so has part of the walls. There's not a piece of furniture intact. You see the occasional body of a Sky Watch Officer and curse Krazic and his vile creation, whatever its true nature may be.

You hear a groan come from one of the bodies and run over to help. It's a young woman; battered and bruised, but still alive. You help her to sit up.

"I have to get home," she mutters. "My mother will be worried. The dragon fruit will need harvesting soon." She seems very disorientated.

You find a strip of cloth and dip it in a nearby puddle of water, so that you can clean the blood and dirt from the woman's face. The cold water seems to bring her to her senses.

"Is it over?" she asks, looking at you with fear in her eyes. "Has it gone?"

You reassure the woman, who tells you her name is Malia, and tell her that now Nimbus is rising you will soon be safely back in Pangaria.

The room shakes with the turbulence of the ascent, which dislodges some of the piles of rubble. The Sky Watch Officer gasps as a large metal face is exposed, along with part of a chest and further down part of a leg and a huge metal foot. It's some kind of metal giant, that is thankfully inert.

You move closer. So, this is what Krazic was working on – a hulking war golem to take to Khul and sell to whichever warlord would pay the highest price. It both saddens and angers you that Pangarian technomancy could be used for such warmongering ends.

You can see from a cavity in the chest where the storm

crystal that powered it was once located, but thankfully it now lies broken. You can't imagine the kind of destruction this monstrosity would wreak if it were fully powered up.

There's a creak and high up you see a small hatch open in the face of the giant. The hatch is just big enough for an angry Goblin face to poke out of. Turn to **370**.

225

You duck skilfully and roll out of the way. The log whooshes by your head.

If Altos is your home isle, turn to **348**. If Altos is not your home isle, turn to **110**.

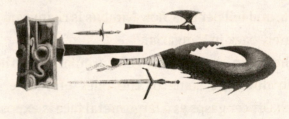

226

Everything looks different from the air, but you listen out for the sound of banging and cussing, and soon manage to guide your hovers to Matix's workshop.

The Goblin pops her head out, grinning from beneath her usual grimy exterior.

"Well, what have you got for me?"

If you have located the Thingie, turn to **125**. If you have obtained a Wotsit, turn to **375**.

You select the item you want to buy. (Deduct the appropriate number of Gold Pieces from your total Gold and add the item to you Adventure Sheet.) As you hand over the coins, you tell the Goblin trader that you're looking into what happened on Nimbus and ask if he knows anything.

"Well, business has been a bit slow since the explosion," he explains. "Everyone's a little nervous about all the extra elemental energy flying around here. But I ain't budging!"

You ask him if he thinks there's anyone you should speak with.

The Goblin sucks his teeth thoughtfully. "Well, there's a Goblin called Hazi who lives on the far side of the market. He used to work at the Citadel on Nimbus. He might know something."

Anyone else?

"You could always go and see Methedus. He's a Stormborn who works over at the mill. He might know a thing or two about the elemental energy that got released."

Now you've got a couple of avenues to explore, but before you set off again you can purchase the other items if you wish. (Update your Adventure Sheet accordingly.)

"Be careful out there," adds the Goblin trader. "There's rumours that the explosion has stirred up some unpleasant beasts. Wouldn't want to lose a good customer like yourself."

Before you head off you notice a Goblin gambling stall. This could be a chance to increase your gold ... or lose it all.

If you want to engage in a game of chance, in the hope of increasing your gold, turn to **304**. If you want to find Hazi's house on the far side of the market, turn to **351**. If you want to head over to see Methedus at the mill, turn to **261**.

228

You give Vizigg the copper ring. He looks delighted. "Aha! Well done, Officer!"

If you have a silver goblet, turn to **115**. If you have a black candle, turn to **6**. If you want to leave the Under-Library and go in search of these items, turn to **26**. If you have given Vizigg all the requested items, turn to **206**.

With a last splintering of wood, the front door finally gives way and you warily enter the house.

Inside, there are papers strewn about and a coat stand has been knocked over. You're about to investigate further when you hear the noise of something *clattering* down the rickety wooden stairs. This is accompanied by *high-pitched laughter.*

Suddenly you see two disc-like creatures, each with four hands sprouting from their sides. They are holding little knives and are cartwheeling towards you with murder in their eyes.

	SKILL	STAMINA
First WHEELIE	6	6
Second WHEELIE	6	6

If you win, turn to **119**.

A Goblin head pokes out of the guts of the bathysphere

A Goblin head pokes out of the guts of the bathysphere, covered in grime and looking very frustrated.

"You don't happen to have a Wotsit on you, do you?" she asks you in an exasperated tone.

You're pretty sure you don't, even if you knew what one was.

"How about a Thingie?"

Still nothing. And you're just as confused.

You explain to her that you have no idea what she's asking for, but you do have a pressing need to commandeer the *Barnacle* in the name of the Sky Watch.

She emerges from the bathysphere, wiping her hands. "Is that right? Well, seeing as this is the only bathysphere that's even partway running right now, Officer, I'd say you need to do a bit more work than just commandeer it."

You apologize for your brusqueness and tell her that you're the only Sky Watch Officer still active on the archipelago and you're trying to find out what happened on Nimbus. You need a way to get down to the island and navigate the rough waters.

Matix looks you up and down appraisingly. "I like the cut of your gib, Officer. At least someone around here is trying to do something and not running around like a headless chicken. Tell you what, if you can find me a Thingie, and either a Doobry or a Wotsit, I can finish repairing the *Barnacle*, and then I'll lend her to you."

She points towards a small contraption that looks like those you've seen at the Goblin flyer ports. "You can charge your hover crystal in that," she says. One Gold Piece per charge. Very reasonable, I'd say."

If you have the Strange Metal Object from the Cirrus Watchhouse, turn to **62**. If not, turn to **2**.

231

You make your way down the left-hand passage. Your senses are alerted when the little glowing fish around you all go into hiding at once. Then you see it. Staring at you through the gloom is the snake-like face of a huge Electric Eel, and it is clearly not happy about its peace being disturbed. You can see elemental energy rippling over its skin. It swims closer to you, sizing you up and deciding whether you are worth the trouble.

If you want to engage the Electric Eel in combat, turn to **41**. If you'd rather not fight the monster fish, turn to **333**.

232

With the bridge now open, you step on to the pleasant

isle of Cirrus, which produces much of the magically enhanced fruit, vegetables and grains that feed Pangaria. You're nervous about what the magical energy released by Nimbus may have done to the vegetation. You look around and spot a plume of blue-green smoke in the distance. You also realize that the local Watchhouse is not too far away. That might be worth visiting for supplies.

To investigate the plume of blue-green smoke, turn to **137**. To investigate the local Watchhouse, turn to **49**.

233

You pluck up the courage and decide to try the Sky Bridge. (If you have Dav with you, he will stay on Cumulus and you will lose your attack and damage bonuses. Adjust this on your Adventure Sheet.)

You step on to the bridge; it sways gently beneath you. Somehow it feels less safe than wearing the hovers. You take a deep breath and, putting one foot in front of the other, begin to cross.

You notice that, although you can see the end of the bridge on Cirrus, part of the bridge near Cumulus is shrouded in cloud. As you approach you can hear a *hissing* sound coming from within. Something long and scaly scythes in and out of the mist. Will you:

Continue into the mist? Turn to **327**.

Return to Daxa and try another route? Turn to **180**.

234

The door finally breaks, and you enter the tower. You find yourself in a relatively bare stone chamber with stairs leading upwards. You begin your ascent. One step *creaks* ominously when you put your weight on it. You hear a faintly audible *click* and darts fly out of the wall at you.

Test Your Skill. If you are Successful, turn to **309**. If you are Unsuccessful, turn to **173**.

235

You take out the storm crystal and look at it; the damage on the inside of the crystal is a miniature version of what you can see all around you. Perhaps you weren't that far off when you thought it looked like the place had been hit by a hurricane.

If you want to explore upstairs, turn to **42**. If you would rather leave and go to the east dock, turn to **74**. If you want to leave and go to Matix's house, turn to **161**.

236

You venture down the half-flooded passageway and come to the body of the Saltwater Crocodile.

If you haven't cut open the creature's stomach and explored its contents, then turn to **183**. If you want to return to Nimbiferous Chamber, turn to **194**.

237

As you slowly creep into the cave you hear the sound that alternates between a *growling* and a *whining*. Something large approaches from out of the shadows, eyes aglow.

If Nemi is with you, turn to **55**. If Nemi is **not** with you, turn to **50**.

238

The spell leaves the chest and the lid sinks down, lifeless once more. Inside you find a flask of fire oil and a piece of paper. You unfold the paper carefully. It looks like a page torn out of a ledger from one of the fishery docks in Incus. A few names are marked on the page, but one name, *Commander Mathias Talliman*, has been circled several times. Scrawled next to it are the words *Where is he?*

You can add the Incus ledger page and the fire oil to your Adventure Sheet. (The fire oil can be used once to light a fire, or it can be used against an opponent at the start of a battle, and will automatically cause your enemy 3 *STAMINA* points of damage.)

You catch sight of yourself in a copper water jug; turn to **177**.

239

You remove *A Sting in the Tale: A Collection of Unexpected Endings* from the shelf. There's a *click* and something shifts. Before you can investigate it, a GIANT SCORPION emerges from behind a bookcase and, tail raised and stinger shining, it skitters towards you.

GIANT SCORPION   *SKILL* 10   *STAMINA* 10

If you win, turn to **373**.

240

You manage to swiftly get behind a tall cabinet. Turn to **162**.

241

You return to the street.

To now head for the rooftops, turn to **117**. To squeeze back down into the storm drain, turn to **79**. To abandon your Coin Bag and continue to the far side of the market, turn to **336**.

242

You head towards the east dock, hoping to find Matix and commandeer one of the bathyspheres to take down to the fallen Nimbus. You realize that you've never piloted one before, but then again, you've done a lot of things you've never done before in the last few hours.

Suddenly the feeling of responsibility and fear washes over you. Your mind is buzzing, but your pace slows. You need a rest. You spot a shed nearby with an empty hammock strung up inside. You try not to think about what might have happened to the fisherman who used it last.

To rest for a few hours, turn to **10**. To continue on to the east dock, turn to **74**.

243

When you reach the Watchhouse, you notice that some grapevines from the local vineyard seem to be growing closer to the building than you remember. You hurry inside.

The emptiness within reminds you of the loss of your friends and fellow recruits in the Sky Watch. You fervently hope that they still might be alive.

You head for the barracks, hoping that some of the recruits' chests might be open so you can search them for any useful supplies.

If Cirrus is your home island, turn to **15**. If Cirrus is not your home island, turn to **123**.

244

You tell Tideus that you don't have any food to give him. "Boo!" he bellows. "Boo! Booooooo!" He then slaps his hands together and prepares to wrestle you.

HUNGRY TIDEUS   *SKILL* 9   *STAMINA* 16

If you manage to reduce the Sea Giant's *STAMINA* score to 6 points or fewer, turn to **267** at once.

245

Unfortunately, it spots you and zooms off. You run after it.
   Test Your Stamina. It you are Successful, turn to **13**. If you are Unsuccessful, turn to **87**.

246

You hurl the fire oil and manage to hit the Goblin War Golem precisely near the Goblin trapped inside who is most afraid of fire – the one controlling the left leg of the contraption. The Goblin panics at the sudden flames and loses control of the leg. In turn, the Golem loses its balance and crashes to the ground. (Deduct 5 points from the War Golem's *STAMINA* score.)
   But before Tideus can finish it off, the mechanical monster picks itself up again. Turn to **326**.

247

"Not your day, is it, Officer?" says the Goblin, pocketing your gold. "Want to try again?"

You decide that it's not worth the risk of losing more.

If you want to head for Hazi's place on the far side of the market, turn to **351**. If you want to head to the mill, turn to **261**. If you have not browsed the nearby stall, and want to, turn to **258**.

248

You duck and roll as a blade swishes over your head. You're not quite agile enough to avoid it, and the blade slices off an ear. (Lose 2 *STAMINA* points.) You stem the bleeding and wonder why anywhere in the Citadel would need a trap to protect it.

You're still wondering this as you walk forward and get slightly scorched by a fireball spat out by a statue embedded in the wall. (Lose 1 more *STAMINA* point.)

Make that traps.

You move ahead extremely cautiously. Turn to **210**.

249

Your boot is well-aimed and strikes the flying eye. Something metal falls off the side of it. The thing emits a high-pitched noise, before flying away up the chimney. You examine what dropped off the contraption. It's a Strange Metal Object. (Add this to your Equipment List.)

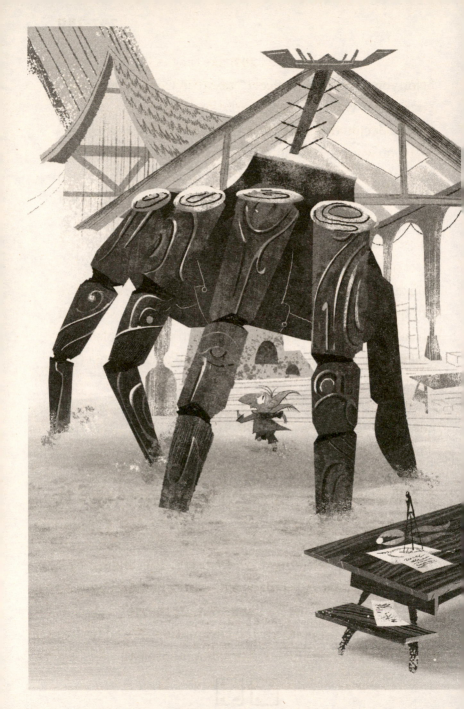

It skitters crab-like across the ground towards you

You're unharmed but can't shake the feeling that you're being watched. But there's no time to dwell on such things right now. There's nothing more to do here, so you leave the Watchhouse. Turn to **335**.

250

The crowd stands back as Nix places the charger against the large metal boulder and pulls the lever on the device. There's a *humming* noise. Nothing happens. He pulls the level up another notch. The *humming* gets louder.

Suddenly the boulder rises into the air. It looks like it's floating, but then it sprouts legs. Oddly, there are five of them. The boulder flips over and you realize what it is – a giant metal hand. The crowd screams and immediately flees at great speed, as does Nix.

You're left alone with the Giant Metal Hand. It skitters crab-like across the ground towards you. It suddenly rears up and you realize it's going to attack.

GIANT METAL HAND　　　　*SKILL 8*　　*STAMINA 11*

Each time you make a successful hit against the Giant Hand it does its battle move, which is to leap at you with all five digits outstretched. Roll one die for each digit; if you roll 1 or 2, the digit hits you for 1 extra *STAMINA* point of damage, but if you roll a 3 to 6, you deflect the blow and the Giant Metal Hand loses 1 *STAMINA* point.

If you win the battle, turn to **108**.

251

Nemi examines the door. "Doesn't look too tough. Let's barge it down together." You ready yourselves. "One, two, THREE!" shouts Nemi.

You both ram the door. *THUNK!* The wood splinters around the lock, and the door flies opens. You head inside.

You find yourself within the familiarity of your own Watchhouse and follow the sound of the *snoring*. It seems to be coming from the small back room off the barracks. As you enter you hear a *whooshing* noise and catch sight of a log heading towards your face.

Test Your Skill. If you are Successful, turn to **225**. If you are Unsuccessful, turn to **160**.

252

You pull the *Barnacle* up to the steps and clamber out. (You must now rely wholly on your own *SKILL* and *STAMINA* score, for as long as you remain out of the bathysphere.) The air pocket encompasses a large section of the Nimbus. You're not sure how long the oxygen will last, but at least the place isn't completely flooded.

"Hey! Hey, you! Help us! Please!"

You see two Sky Watch Officers heading towards you. One has been hurt and is being supported by the other. They are being pursued by bouncing spherical creatures covered in spines. You must come to the aid of your Sky Watch comrades. Fight the Spinefish two at a time.

	SKILL	STAMINA
First AMPHIBIOUS SPINEFISH	7	6
Second AMPHIBIOUS SPINEFISH	6	7
Third AMPHIBIOUS SPINEFISH	6	6

If an Amphibious Spinefish lands a hit against you, roll one die; if you roll a 5 or a 6, then the attack will cause you to lose 2 additional *STAMINA* points, as the Spinefish's spines are coated with a toxic secretion.

If you win, turn to **283**.

253

You rub the lemon over the page. Nothing happens.

If you want to light the lamp and hold the page close to the glass, turn to **23**. If you want to leave the tower and head north-east back to the maze of workshops and laboratories, turn to **111**.

254

The tentacles burst out of Caleb's chest like the blossoming of a terrifying black flower. They start slithering about, searching for prey. Caleb is beyond pain now, thankfully – but you are not!

OCTOBEAST   SKILL 7   STAMINA 6

If you win, turn to **47**.

255

You reach the north end of Cirrus and look for the Goblin flyer which normally takes the inhabitants on to the other islands. You eventually find the flyer, but its balloon is deflated, and its Goblin pilot is rummaging angrily in his tool bag whilst muttering to himself.

You approach him carefully. Turn to **346**.

256

You leave the Citadel in the bathysphere.

If you haven't explored the caves yet, turn to **85**. To explore the seabed, turn to **394**.

257

You ask Yurik where you can find Elder Technomancer Vizigg's home.

"To the west, in an old bell tower. Right, I gotta get going, Officer. Good luck!"

He takes a full vial and passes it to you; it's a Greater Potion of Might. (Add the Greater Potion of Might to your Adventure Sheet; it will raise your Attack Strength by 2 points for the duration of one battle, and will also restore 2 *STAMINA* points. Also gain 1 *LUCK* point.) He then heads back into the workshop.

(Write the codeword **Vizigg** on your Adventure Sheet.)

You decide where to go next. There's the residential area, which is a little greener and quieter, and the workshop and laboratories section of the island, which is busier and more closely built-up.

You also notice a nearby device which charges up storm crystals. You can use it to get charge and return to Matix in Incus when you need to.

Do you want to head west, towards where the residents of Asperitas live (turn to **293**), or north, further into the maze of workshops and laboratories (turn to **111**)?

258

You browse a nearby stall.

You can buy some bread for 1 Gold Piece (which will restore 2 *STAMINA* points). or an apple pie for 2 Gold Pieces (which will restore 3 *STAMINA* points) or a Calming Potion for 2 Gold Pieces.

Choose what you want to buy and deduct the appropriate number of Gold Pieces from your Adventure Sheet.

If you want to head for Hazi's place on the far side of the market, turn to **351**. If you want to head to the mill, turn to **261**. If you want to engage in a game of chance and maybe increase your gold, turn to **304**.

259

As the body of the Great White Squark drifts down into the depths, you manage to activate the *Barnacle*'s suction tube on the right pincer and capture yourself a piece of fresh calamari. (Add this to your Provisions List. It will restore up to 3 *STAMINA* when eaten.)

You feel the water vibrate around you. You brace yourself, but nothing appears, and eventually the vibrations cease.

If you want to continue exploring the surface, turn to **120**. If you want to dive below, turn to **203**.

260

You see before you a fellow Sky Watch Officer who let his comrades walk into danger, and then tried to kill you. But can you really murder one of your own? Your brief hesitation gives him time to swing his sword upwards towards your leg. You move swiftly and the blade only deals a glancing blow (lose 1 *STAMINA* point). You bring your sword down and finish off the coward.

You search his body and find 1 Gold Piece and a Calming Potion. (Add these to your Adventure Sheet.) In his pocket you also find a crumpled note. It reads:

Whatever you do, don't go to the Nimbus this morning.
Your friend,
Paxlo

You recognize the name as being that of a Goblin who works over on Asperitas, the island of technomancy. You also find an Apple.

(Add these to your Adventure Sheet, making a note that the Apple will restore up to 2 *STAMINA* points when eaten.)

You leave the Watchhouse.

If you have not already visited the Great Waterfall, and want to do so now, turn to **328**. If you would prefer to find the nearest flyer, so you can get off this island, turn to **361**.

261

You make your way around the edge of the market, heading towards the mill. The ground begins to rumble beneath your feet. Market-goers start sprinting for cover and before you can ask what the fuss is about, the only shopkeeper left nearby shouts "RUN!" before quickly pulling down the wooden shutter on his shop with a loud *clonk*.

If Dav is with you, turn to **399**. If Dav is not with you, turn to **311**.

262

You struggle against whatever is restraining you, fervently trying to reach the surface. Just as your lungs are about to collapse, you manage to break free (lose 2 *STAMINA* points) and swim for the shore. Turn to **314**.

263

You vanquish the creature, but nothing seems to have changed. You look at the shelf and select a book you haven't already tried:

Tooth and Claw: Famous Fights to the Death	Turn to **45**.
Winged Menaces: Death from Above	Turn to **89**.
A Sting in the Tale: A Collection of Unexpected Endings	Turn to **239**.
Denizens of the Deep: Aquatic Beasts and How to Kill Them	Turn to **341**.

If you don't want to pick up any of the books, then there's nowhere else to explore in the library, so turn to **92** to return to the Nimbiferous Chamber.

264

You follow the beautiful voices as they sing their haunting melody out into the storm. Then suddenly, through the wind and the rain, you see them. Beautiful female figures sitting on the rocks ahead – human to the waist, with long colourful fish tails that shine with an iridescent light. The figures are brushing their hair and giving voice to the most beautiful melody you've ever heard. It seems to go right through you, making your skin tingle.

You move the *Barnacle* closer. There's a sickening metallic *crunch* as your poor bathysphere crashes against the rocks. You open the hatch and crawl out, weakly. As you lie dazed on the cold, wet ground, you wonder what rocks are doing in the middle of the ocean anyway.

As the creatures slither over to look at you, their beautiful faces all smiles and laughter, you think you are safe. But their smiles turn to grimaces as their fangs lengthen and their skin turns black. The last thing you remember is teeth. So many teeth.

Your adventure is over.

265

You put Methedus's shard on the ground and stand back. The shard starts to spin and rises into the air, drawing out the unstable elemental energy from the Canidor. Flapps starts to shrink in size. The glow leaves his eyes and his fur stops sparking.

Flapps licks your face, bounds out of the cave and takes off, heading for the Cloudkin farm. (Remove Methedus's Shard from your Adventure Sheet.)

You find a longsword, lying amongst the rocks and dirt at the back of the cave. (Record the longsword on your Adventure Sheet. If you use the longsword in battle, you may increase your Attack Strength by 1 point.)

You leave the cave.

If you want to investigate the Goblin flyer, turn to **361**. If you haven't been to the Watchhouse and want to go there now, turn to **40**.

266

The Octopus slithers away through a gap in the floor. The fisherman coughs and splutters as he struggles to catch his breath. He tells you his name is Caleb. You ask him how he came to be in such a predicament.

"I'd just brought my boat up after the Nimbus fell

and the storms set in," Caleb wheezes. "I was cleaning her hull and suddenly I feel something drop on my head and . . . not sure of much after that, or how long I'd been stumbling around for, but somehow I made it back here."

Caleb's breathing starts to settle. He thanks you for your help and gives you 2 Gold Pieces. (Record these on your Adventure Sheet and gain 1 *LUCK* point.)

"Ever since we saw that last shipwreck, nothing's gone right," he mutters. "I mean it was there in the name, *Doombringer*. Doesn't exactly bode well, does it?"

To press Caleb for more information about the *Doombringer*, turn to **17**. To leave Caleb to rest and continue to the east dock, turn to **74**.

267

"OK, OK, yous got me," says Tideus, holding up his hands. "I owes yous an' yer little ball fingy one favour."

He hands you a conch shell, which you seize with one of the bathysphere's mechanical claws. "Blows on dis when yous needs Tideus."

(Add the Conch to your Equipment List.)

The Sea Giant then opens the Citadel door and

gestures for you to enter.

"I is gonna take a nap an' be nice an' ready fors my next fight!"

He plonks himself down next to the door and soon starts snoring loudly. It sounds like a cross between whale song and a localized underwater explosion. In between being buffeted about by the currents produced by his snores, you manage to enter the Citadel. Turn to **377**.

268

You hit the door hard, but it doesn't budge an inch.

You have a feeling your body will break before the door does. (Lose 1 more *STAMINA* point and 1 *SKILL* point from the injuries you have sustained trying to break into the bell tower.)

You decide to give up, which is probably what you should have done in the first place. Turn to **111**.

269

On entering the mill, you can see that the circle Methedus was floating above is covered in strange symbols. You ask what exactly he's doing, fearing that he may somehow be involved in the fall of the Nimbus.

"When the explosion happened, there was a Stormborn present," he explains. "I felt their energy and I also felt it leave after the Nimbus fell. Perhaps they were there when it happened and fled from the scene or maybe they're trapped down there, I don't know. I was trying to reconnect with their energy, but no matter what I do, I can't."

He's telling the truth. You feel it in your bones.

Methedus passes you a small crystal. It looks like a blank version of the one you have in your hovers.

"You might need this. You seem like the type that gets themselves in danger. There are a lot of nasty energies around and this will withdraw them from an infected creature, just as long as it's not too far gone. Once it's been taken over entirely, the crystal won't work. One use only, I'm afraid." (Add Methedus's shard to your Adventure Sheet.)

There's nothing more left to do here.

If you want to look for Hazi in the market, and haven't done so already, turn to **351**.

If you want to find the local Goblin flyer and head on for the other islands, turn to **26**.

Two Harpies descend on you from out of the sky

270

Feeling a little more in control of your hovers now, you head in the direction of Asperitas. This is the island of technomancy, the mechanical magic that underpins the levitation enchantments of the archipelago. From the air the island is a mess of workshops and laboratories from which a cacophony of *clangs* and *thunks* mixed with *bubbling* and *fizzing* noises can be heard.

You're close to landing when you hear a loud *birdlike scream* and two Harpies descend on you from out of the sky. You have no choice but to fight them together, before you can land.

	SKILL	STAMINA
First HARPY	7	6
Second HARPY	6	6

If you manage to kill the first Harpy, you get a chance to pull the second one to the ground. Roll one die; if you roll a 1 to 3, then you cause it 2 *STAMINA* points of damage instantly, but if you roll 4 to 6, you cause it 4 *STAMINA* points of damage.

If you win, turn to **156**.

271

The scarecrow explodes in a ball of straw and cabbages. You breathe a sigh of relief. You've heard that cabbage leaves can be soothing, so you take two with you just in case. (Record the cabbage leaves on your Adventure Sheet, noting that each will restore 2 *STAMINA* points when used.)

Now you can reach the little shed, you find a small hand axe and a Calming Potion inside. (Record these items on your Adventure Sheet.)

If you want to head to the north of Cirrus and search for a Goblin flyer, turn to **255**. If you want to visit the local Watchhouse, if you haven't already done so, turn to **49**.

272

Vizigg laughs so hard that he has to sit down to regain his breath.

"Well, you've found them, Officer. I'm the one who brought the Nimbus down. But believe me, if I had not done so, things would've been a lot worse for Pangaria. These measures I took might have been extreme, but they were necessary in order to protect our archipelago and the world beyond."

You ask him what happened.

"You have taken a great risk in coming down here, and I'm sure it was no easy task, so I will assume that your intentions are honourable. As you are aware, Officer, I helped maintain the technomancy that keeps Pangaria aloft. When I retired, I kept my honorary title, but Krazic, one of my brightest and most ambitious apprentices, eventually became Chief Engineer, responsible for the day-to-day running and maintaining of the technomancy.

"I received word that Krazic had been taking an interest in Commander Mathias Talliman, a survivor brought to Incus from a wrecked Khulian warship. Together they had hatched a plan to use the secrets of Pangarian technomancy to develop weapons of war within Krazic's private workshop in the Nimbus."

You tell him that you have discovered some of this yourself, during your investigations.

Vizigg looks impressed. "Then you are a better Sky Watch officer than most!" He fiddles with his wrist contraption and the net loosens and retracts, returning to the sheath on his arm. You rub some feeling back into your limbs.

If you have the Codeword **Boreas** on your Adventure Sheet, turn to **98**. If not, turn to **284**.

273

The Goblin begrudgingly hands over your winnings. You hope to play again, but the Goblin waves you away: "You think I'm made of gold, eh?"

If you want to head for Hazi's place on the far side of the market, turn to **351**. If you want to head to the mill, turn to **261**. If you have not yet browsed the stalls of the market traders, and would like to, turn to **258**.

274

You decide to search for any clues that might tell you what happened in the Renard house, but find nothing of note. That is until you happen upon a small, sparsely furnished, and surprisingly neat room. This would seem completely normally were it not for the destruction and chaos you have seen everywhere else in the house.

If you decide that the neat little room needs further examination, turn to **296**. If you want to leave and go towards Matix's home, turn to **161**. If you want to leave, and head to the east dock and the bathysphere shed, turn to **74**.

275

Your sword falls short and hits the pipe, knocking the fleeing Giant Cockroach out into the mud. It *hisses* at you and then makes a strange high-pitched *shrieking* sound. Another two cockroaches promptly emerge from the pipe and join it. The Giant Cockroaches advance on you hungrily.

	SKILL	STAMINA
First GIANT COCKROACH	5	5
Second GIANT COCKROACH	6	5
Third GIANT COCKROACH	6	6

You must fight the three overgrown insects at the same time. If you win turn to **367**.

276

You hurl the fire oil, but it hits the Golem's kneecap and bounces off, setting fire to a pile of rubble before flaming out. Turn to **326**.

"Good work, Officer," says the Cloudkin farmer, who introduces herself as Nemi. "I hate to take out a Cloudkin, but that one was too far gone."

You tell her that you are investigating what happened on Nimbus, as the last member of the Sky Watch still in Pangaria.

"Hmm, you might not be the last one," says Nemi thoughtfully. "I went by the Watchhouse just before the explosion and I heard snoring coming from inside."

Seems that someone else didn't make the meeting. You should probably look into that.

"Right, well, thank you for your help, Officer. I'd better clean this place up," says Nemi, looking around wearily. "You're welcome to keep the Cloudkin staff. And could you keep an eye out for Flapps, my best Canidor? Most of the Canidors scattered when the explosion occurred and haven't been seen since. I'm really worried about him. Hopefully, he's in hiding, he always liked the area up by the Great Waterfall."

She reaches into her pocket. "This might come in useful too," she says, pressing a pear into your hand. (Add the pear to your Provisions and make a note that it will restore up to 2 *STAMINA* points when eaten.)

(If you choose to use the wooden Cloudkin staff in battle, you must reduce your Attack Strength by 1 point, against opponents that aren't Cloudkin, as it is more cumbersome to use than your short sword. For now add the staff to your Weapons list.)

If you want to go towards the Altos Watchhouse, turn to **40**. If you want to go towards the Great Waterfall, turn to **328**.

278

The fireball bounces off your sword on to your boot and sets fire to your foot. (Lose 2 *STAMINA* points.) By the time you've put the flames out, the strange eyeball has flown away up the chimney.

You can't shake the feeling that you're being watched. But there's no time to dwell on such things right now – you need to get moving.

(Write the codeword **Eye-Spy** on your Adventure Sheet.)

Choosing something you've not already tried, will you:

Search your chest?	Turn to **217**.
See what Silas found earlier?	Turn to **134**.
Leave the Watchhouse?	Turn to **335**.

279

You decide where to explore next in the Renard homestead.

If you want to explore upstairs, turn to **42**. If you want to leave and go to east dock and the bathysphere shed, turn to **74**. If you want to leave and go to Matix's house, turn to **161**.

280

You climb out of the *Barnacle* and make your way to the upper door. You press an ear to the wood. A dull *moaning* comes from the other side. Another creature, perhaps? A terrible monster? The walking dead? You shove open the door forcefully, prepared to meet whatever horrors await you on the other side. Turn to **188**.

281

You know that occasionally the fishermen have been known to rescue shipwreck survivors from the tempestuous waters below Pangaria and, when possible, return them home. Once in a blue moon a survivor will need to be brought up to the archipelago for healing and ends up becoming a permeant resident of Pangaria. You ask Caleb if he knows any more about the survivor.

"He was pretty close to death when we got to him," recalls Caleb. "We had to bring him up here or he wouldn't have made it."

If you want to ask him the man's name, turn to **144**. If you want to ask him if there's anything else he knows about the *Doombringer*, and you haven't done so already, turn to **33**. To leave Caleb in peace and head for the east dock to look for Matix, turn to **295**.

282

You show Hazi the storm crystal shard you picked up on Cirrus. He examines it closely.

"This doesn't look like it's from one of the Nimbus storm crystals, but it's definitely come from something very large. Much larger than you would find used in most of the technomancy in Pangaria."

He sniffs the black substance on the shard. "Oil!" he exclaims. "This type is most popular on Asperitas. How strange."

He hands the storm crystal shard back to you. "If I were you, I'd take this to Methedus over at the mill. He might be able to tell you more about where it came from." Turn to **185**.

283

The Spinefish deflate with a sad squeaky noise.

"Thank you. How long have you been stuck here?" says the uninjured Officer whilst his injured friend sits down to rest.

You tell them that you've just arrived in a bathysphere to try to help the Nimbus.

To ask them what happened to the Nimbus, turn to **77**. If you want to ask what's wrong with the injured officer, turn to **356**. To ask them if there are many other survivors, turn to **197**.

284

Now it's your chance to ask the ancient Goblin a few questions.

To ask what has befallen him, turn to **11**. If you want to ask him why the Nimbus crashed, turn to **82**. If you want to ask about the ward on the Great Hall door, turn to **338**. If you want to ask what Vizigg is doing with the broken storm crystals, turn to **59**.

285

You hurl the Calming Potion towards Flapps, who grabs it in his teeth. The bottle breaks and the liquid pours into his mouth. It works quickly and Flapps starts to shrink in size. The glow leaves his eyes and his fur stops sparking.

Flapps licks your face, before bounding out of the cave and taking off, heading in the direction of the Cloudkin farm. (Add 1 point to your *LUCK* score.)

You find a longsword, lying amongst the rocks and dirt at the back of the cave.

(Record the longsword in the Weapons box on your Adventure Sheet. If you use the longsword in battle, you may increase your Attack Strength by 1 point.)

Leaving the cave, if you want to investigate the Goblin flyer, turn to **361**; if you haven't been to the Watchhouse and want to go there now, turn to **40**.

286

You run forward and sweep up the elderly Goblin. You manage to shelter his fragile little body with your own, but some of the falling debris hits you. (Lose 2 *STAMINA* points.) Turn to **216**.

287

You slip round to the back of the house. The door is slightly ajar. You push it open forcefully and see a terrified Goblin almost jump out of his skin. He's dressed in Asperitas worker clothes and you also notice he's wearing a belt with an ornate brass buckle with a *P* engraved on it. You tell him to stay still, but he shouts out a few strange words, unlocks the front door and bolts outside.

You hear something clattering down the rickety wooden stairs, accompanied by high-pitched laughter. Suddenly you see two disc-like creatures, each with four hands sprouting from their sides. They are holding little knives and are cartwheeling towards you with murder in their eyes.

	SKILL	STAMINA
First WHEELIE	6	6
Second WHEELIE	6	6

If you win, turn to **358**.

288

The corridor ahead seems familiar and you remember it's one that leads to the Citadel library. Maybe there are more survivors in there.

The corridor slopes downwards towards the library door. There's waist-high water around it. You're just about to open the door when you are knocked off your feet by a swishing tail.

You scramble on to a bench. A dark shadow slices through the water. It's a huge Saltwater Crocodile. There's no way you're going to get into the library without dispatching this beast.

If you want to fight it, turn to **398**. If you want to run back to the Nimbiferous Chamber, turn to **48**.

289

With an enormous shudder, the creature crashes to the ground. Slowly the market-goers return and start poking at the huge corpse.

"Nice work, Officer!"

"Do you think this can be roasted? Stewed, maybe."

"Worth a try!"

The stallholder cautiously raises his shutter.

"Well I never, you got it! Here, take some dried stink fruit and silk cloth on the house."

(You can add the silk cloth and the 2 dried stink fruit to your Adventure Sheet. The dried stink fruit will restore up to 2 *STAMINA* points each when consumed.)

You keep heading on for the mill. Turn to **64**.

"I'll crack open that brass bubble and have squishy hooman for lunc**

You navigate to the main Citadel door. You're just gliding the bathysphere up the steps when you feel vibrations so strong that they push you back down. As you try to approach again, you see two large green legs like tree trunks come into view. You look up and see a grumpy-looking sea giant who plops himself down in front of the Citadel door, barring your way.

It could've been a lot worse. Sea Giants have had a largely neutral relationship with the Pangarians for many generations. They've even been known to trade with the fishermen. Still, they can be unpredictable and aggressive, so you approach with care.

"Was it you wot woke me with yer crashin' about?" he bellows when he sees you. "I is having a nice dream, when BOOM a dead Great White Squark hits me inna face. And I fink yous and yer little brass ball knows all about dis!"

You apologize to the Sea Giant.

"Course, den I has breakfast in bed," he says with a laugh that nearly knocks the *Barnacle* over. "But now I is peckish again." He stretches out his arms and flexes his muscles, which are the size of barrels. "Or maybes I needs a good wrestle with somefink. Or maybes I need food, ana wrestle. Yeah dat's it! You, me an' your little ball thingie, let's go!"

You tell him that normally you'd love to wrestle, but you need to get into the Citadel urgently.

"And Tideus needs to wrestle urgently! Tell you wot, if we wrestle and yous win, I'll owe yous a favour. If yous lose,

I'll crack open that brass bubble and have squishy hooman for lunch! But maybe if yous gotta snack for Tideus, Tideus go a little easier on yous."

The Sea Giant requires 4 *STAMINA* points' worth of food. If you have it and want to give it to him, turn to **166**. If you don't have food or don't want to share it with the Giant, turn to **244**.

291

You decide that a cooling swim would be most welcome.

If Altos is your home island, turn to **31**, but if Altos is not your home island, turn to **322**.

292

You descend a couple of floors and then come to a dingy tunnel. It's lit with small torches. Someone's been this way recently.

You move ahead. Suddenly there's a *whooshing* noise at around head height.

Test Your Skill. If you are Successful, turn to **34**. If you are Unsuccessful, turn to **248**.

293

You decide to head west to the residential area. Everywhere you go there are groups of Goblins, humans, the occasional Stormborn, and other species, discussing what happened at the Nimbus. The Goblins are taking what happened very personally, as it seems to be their technomancy which somehow failed and caused the crash.

You are moving down an alleyway when you hear a *buzzing* sound.

If you have the codeword **Eye-Spy** written on your Adventure Sheet, turn to **317**. If not, turn to **357**.

294

You ram the door and it gives, but doesn't break. (Lose 2 *STAMINA* points, as you injure your shoulder in the process.)

If you want to try ramming the door again, *Test Your Stamina* once more, subtracting 2 from the dice roll if you have an axe or club-like weapon with you; if you pass the test, turn to **234**, but if you fail the test, turn to **268**.

295

Caleb seems like he could do with some rest. You're about to go when he starts choking, as if he's swallowed something. You go to help him.

He pulls at his shirt, exposing his chest, and to the horror of you both, tentacles can be seen moving under his skin. The creature on his head must've laid something inside him!

He *gurgles* and cries out as his skin starts to heave and stretch as whatever is inside him fights to get out. His eyes plead with you to end his torment.

If you want to put Caleb out of his misery, turn to **86**. If you would rather wait and see what happens, turn to **254**.

296

As you explore the little room, your eye is drawn to a glint under the bed. You crawl under and find a small Brass Button that looks like it belongs to a uniform of some kind; perhaps military. You suspect that this is maybe where Commander Talliman was staying. (You can add the brass button to your Equipment List.)

As you are pulling yourself out from under the bed, you notice a tiny bit of paper sticking out from under the skirting boards. You try to pull it out with your fingertips.

Test Your Luck. If you are Lucky, turn to **153**. If you are Unlucky, turn to **366**.

297

The contraption emits a high-pitched noise and sends a small fireball flying toward Silas. You launch yourself in front of your friend with your Short Sword outstretched.

Test Your Skill. If you are Successful, turn to **189**. If you are Unsuccessful, turn to **278**.

298

You don't see Cumulus at first, you smell it. The scents drift up to you from the numerous stalls and vendors who trade their wares in the large markets that dominate the island. The soft, spicy smells of gingerbread biscuits and cinnamon milk pudding mingle with the pungent aroma of stink fruit and sizzling fish steaks.

The smells of home bring a tear to your eye, and your mind drifts as you wonder if Cumulus is destined to suffer the same fate as Nimbus. You can already see the air around where the other island once was crackling with a strange elemental energy. Whatever brought the island down must have been incredibly powerful.

A *humming* jolts you from your musings, and the hovers begin to shudder. You tense your shoulders and move your upper body as you try to glide yourself down towards a safe and soft landing before the storm crystal's energy runs out.

Test Your Skill. If you are Successful, turn to **12**. If you are Unsuccessful, turn to **138**.

299

You start to follow the tracks along the bank. After a while the paw prints become muddy scuffs on the rocks leading to a cave hidden behind the waterfall.

If you want to enter the cave, turn to **237**. If you want to turn back and head for the Goblin flyer instead, turn to **361**.

300

You disorientate and weaken the Goblins controlling the legs. The War Golem topples to the ground.

(Deduct half the War Golem's remaining *STAMINA* points, rounding halves up.) Turn to **100**.

301

You try the handle of the Great Hall door. The ward around it pushes you back (lose 1 *STAMINA* point).

If you want to go back to the half-flooded area near the library, turn to **236**. If you want to return to the bathysphere, turn to **136**. If you decide to explore the kitchens, if you haven't already, turn to **9**. If you want to return to Vizigg, turn to **52**.

302

You manage to dispatch the Howl Cat, but you can't help feeling like someone sent it after you. You decide where to go next.

If you have the codeword **Vizigg** written on your Adventure Sheet, turn to **126**. If not, turn to **214**.

303

With a shake of its few remaining heads, the Dragon Fruit Tree sinks its roots back into the earth and becomes still again. The little dragon heads close their eyes and start to snore gently. The old woman looks relieved.

"Thank you, Officer," says the woman, who introduces herself as Maude, also known as "Maude the Mauler" from her adventuring days. "Good job you turned up when you did, I wasn't looking forward to trying to give those little fellows the old one-two punch." (Add 1 point to your *LUCK* score.)

Maude asks about what's happened over at the Nimbus. Her daughter is in the Sky Watch and went over there for the meeting. Maude is very worried about what might have happened to her.

If you want to tell her the truth, that you don't know, turn to **24**. If you want to tell a white lie and reassure her that everything is all right, turn to **329**.

304

You approach one of the gambling stalls. "Win or lose it all on the roll of a dice!" shouts the Goblin running the stall. "Roll a five or six to win! Double your money. What are you willing to bet, Officer?"

You can bet 1, 2 or 3 Gold Pieces. Then roll one die. If you roll a 5 or 6, you win and double the amount of Gold Piece you bet. If you roll 1 to 4, you lose your stake.

If you win, turn to **273**. If you lose, turn to **247**.

You head towards the light. As you get closer, you see the stranded boat. The fisherman has a lamp lit and he's pulling the shutter back and forth to create the winking effect.

"I heard you surface," he says. "Wanted to make sure you found me. Any luck with the conductor?"

You give him the Brass Rod, hoping it's what he was after. He looks pleased.

"Thank you, Officer. I'll have my boat up and out of here in no time now."

He scrambles up the mast and fits the conductor. The storm crystals fire up and the boat begins to rise out of the water. But before he disappears out of sight, the fisherman throws you some dried crab meat and a Potion of Might.

(There is enough dried crab meat to restore up to 3 *STAMINA* points when eaten. The Potion of Might will add 2 points to your Attack Strength for the duration of one battle only. Also gain 2 *LUCK* points for helping the fisherman. Update your Adventure Sheet accordingly.)

You watch the boat disappear upwards through the storm. Now it's time for you to continue your adventures. Do you want to:

Follow the sound of the singing?   Turn to **264**.
Dive back to the caves if you haven't
finished exploring them?   Turn to **85**.
Or dive towards the large dim shape?   Turn to **191**.

306

You step inside the Watchhouse and follow the sound of the snoring. It seems to be coming from the small back room off the barracks. As you enter you hear a *whooshing* noise and catch sight of a log heading towards your face.

Test Your Skill. If you are Successful, turn to **225**. If you are Unsuccessful, turn to **160**.

307

You can't let your coin bag be taken by this thieving beast! You give chase.

The Cockroach dashes down an alleyway. You follow and come to a dead end. You look around to see where it could have scurried off to, and see a broken storm drain grate, which you might be able to squeeze through, and some steps leading up to the rooftops of some small ramshackle houses.

If you want to try the storm drain, turn to **171**. If you decide to head for the rooftops, turn to **117**.

308

You show the fishermen the ledger page you found on Cirrus.

"It's from here," one of the men confirms, peering at it closely. "Don't recognize that name though. It's no one from Incus. Might be something to do with that ship from the mainland that went down a few months back. Don't know much about it. Maybe ask around."

To look for Matix at the east dock, turn to **242**. To head

A huge, worm-like creature erupts from the ground

for Matix's home in northern Incus, turn to **161**.

309

You successfully defect the darts with your cloak. Luckily, it's reinforced with fine light wires, making it very durable. You continue upwards, unsurprised that someone like Elder Technomancer Vizigg would have traps in his home. You reach a door. Turn to **83**.

310

The cold water reminds you of what's waiting for the Nimbus if you fail in your task – a watery grave! The water ripples around you, but nothing disturbs your swim. Turn to **73**.

311

You can see the earth bucking and cracking as something burrows through the soil towards you, sending market stalls flying.

With hands shaking, you select your best weapon as a huge, worm-like creature erupts from the ground. It seems to have no eyes, but it makes up for that with the number of glistening fangs it has in its huge, gaping mouth, which is heading straight for you.

TUNNELLER BEAST　　　*SKILL 8*　　　*STAMINA 9*

If you win, turn to **289**.

You direct the *Barnacle* forwards through the storm-tossed water, searching for any evidence of the Nimbus. The waves toss you about and you can't help but vomit into the copper bucket that Matix helpfully provided. (Lose 1 *STAMINA* point.) After that you start to feel a little better.

You see a small light object on a wave ahead of you. You get closer and realize that it's a Goblin-made pie. You wonder what kind of pastry the Goblins use, because their snacks are certainly durable!

Suddenly a tentacle reaches up and snatches the pie.

A great monster rises from the water and makes for the bathysphere. With the head and upper body of a monstrous shark, and the tentacle-covered lower body of a giant squid, this is the Great White Squark and it wants you as its next meal. Taking a firm hold of the *Barnacle*'s controls, you prepare to battle the sea monster, using the craft's mechanical claws.

GREAT WHITE SQUARK   SKILL 9   STAMINA 10

If you win, turn to **259**.

313

You look around the room. It's not just one room but several knocked into one. There are various workbenches and metalworking tools and pieces of equipment all over the place. It looks like the floor of the rooms above have been removed to create an extra high ceiling. Nearby are metal frames and ladders, suggesting that something very big was being worked on in here. There is also what looks like a large central platform, and from the lever nearby it looks like it could have been raised and lowered.

You start scavenging. You find a black candle and a Potion of Proficiency. (Add these to your Adventure Sheet. When you drink the potion, you may ignore any penalties you suffer from using your weapon of choice and add 2 points to your Attack Strength for the duration of one battle only.)

You wonder what to do next.

To climb back down to Halleck in the room below, turn to **43**. To test the lever, turn to **143**.

314

You reach the shore, vowing to never go for a swim again!

If you want to walk along the bank to get closer to the Great Waterfall, turn to **75**. If you want to go back and head for the Watchhouse instead, if you haven't been there already, turn to **40**.

315

You pick up the sketches and realize with a shiver that they're drawings of you. There's even one of you walking around Asperitas that must have been drawn quite recently.

You can also see notes that detail your movements around the islands. Whoever lives in this house has been very interested in what you've been up to.

You're filled with rage. You look at the contraption charging the Eye-Spies and see that it regulates the level of charge the storm crystals are receiving.

Do you want to try to overload the charge and destroy the Eye-Spies (turn to **389**), or would you prefer to explore the ground floor, if you haven't already done so (turn to **182**)? Alternatively, you can leave the house by turning to **149**.

316

Wrenching on the controls, you manage to move the *Barnacle* away from the falling rocks. The rockfall ceases, but the tunnel ahead is now blocked. There's nothing for it but to go back the way you came and explore elsewhere.

To take right fork, if you haven't already, turn to **101**. To head for the large dim shape, turn to **191**.

317

You recognize that sound; it's the same as you heard in the Cirrus Watchhouse! And sure enough there's another flying metal-and-glass eye watching you from above. You watch it, in turn, from the corner of your eye until it flies off. You decide to follow it.

Roll one die. If you roll a 1 or 2, turn to **76**. If you roll 3 or 4, turn to **142**. If you roll a 5 or 6, turn to **339**.

318

You hurl the fire oil towards the Goblin War Golem.

Test Your Luck. If you are Lucky, turn to **246**. If you are Unlucky, turn to **276**.

319

You quickly identify a good hiding place and fling yourself towards it.

Test Your Luck. If you are Lucky, turn to **240**. If you are Unlucky, turn to **97**.

320

You decide to visit Cirrus, the farming isle, using your hovers. Daxa charges them up, and with a running jump you take off into the air, leaving the markets of Cumulus behind you.

(If you have Dav with you, he will stay on Cumulus and you will lose your attack and damage bonuses. Adjust this on your Adventure Sheet.) Turn to **105**.

"I didn't think you were going to make it!"

A familiar voice breaks you from your thoughts. It's Silas, an old friend of yours and the best vine wrangler in the whole of Cirrus. "I saw the explosion from here. What happened?" But you have no idea, and those who do have just plummeted into the Ocean of Tempests far below.

You touch your badge sadly as you realize that you may be the only member of the Sky Watch left in Pangaria. Sadness gives way to a new resolve. You're going to find out what happened to Nimbus before the rest of Pangaria starts to fall from the sky.

If you can charge up Halleck's hovers, you will have a valuable piece of equipment at your disposal. You've also managed to keep hold of his Coin Bag. You're pretty sure that he won't mind you borrowing it in the line of duty. (Add 10 Gold Pieces to your Adventure Sheet.)

You check your waist; your trusty short sword is still there. You get the feeling you might need it. (Add the short sword to your Weapons List on your Adventure Sheet.)

"I admire your resolve, my friend," says Silas, supportively slapping you on the back. "I'd better come with you and bring my best pitchfork. Something out there clearly wants to keep you alive and I aim to help it. At least whilst you're on Cirrus. How about we investigate the plume of blue-green smoke coming from that far field? I don't like the look of that one bit."

Silas's support is heartening. As long as he is travelling with you, you may add 2 points when calculating your Attack Strength, you may increase any damage you cause by 1 point, and you may reduce any damage you suffer in battle by 1 point. (Make a note of this on your Adventure Sheet.)

"Right," says Silas. "Where are we off to?"

If you want to go to the local Watchhouse to search for supplies, turn to **49**. If you want to investigate the plume of blue-green smoke, turn to **137**.

322

You dive into the lake. For a few moments the feel of its cooling waters closing over you is refreshing and delightful. Until, that is, you feel something grasp your ankle.

Roll one die. If you roll a 1 or 2, turn to **154**. If you roll a 3 or 4, turn to **262**. If you roll a 5 or 6, turn to **359**.

323

When you finally reach the flyer port, you find a crowd of annoyed Incus residents milling about the place. You push your way through to speak to the pilot.

"The flyers have just been locked down by the island governors," he explains. "They won't allow us to fly our routes until further notice."

You tell him that you're on official duty for the Sky Watch.

"I'm sorry, but unless you have special paperwork from your commander, you're not getting on a flyer," says the pilot, resolutely crossing his arms.

Looks like you'll have to rely on your hovers. You go to charge up your hovers' storm crystal in the charging station. You put 1 Gold Piece into the slot.

Nothing happens.

"It's broken. Sorry," says the pilot.

You ask for your money back.

"I'll need that in writing," he says, a trifle too smugly. "I'm not responsible for malfunctioning technomancy, Officer."

(Deduct 1 Gold Piece, if you haven't done so already.)

Clearly you are going to have to find another way to leave the island, so you head north towards Matix's home. Turn to **161**.

324

You toss Tideus the Potion of Power. He catches it in his mouth and swallows it down. He looks down at his enormous blue hands and balls his fists excitedly.

(Increased both Tideus's *SKILL* score by 1 point and his *STAMINA* score by 3 points, and make a note of these adjustments on your Adventure Sheet.)

"Tideus feel mor powerful! Wot else yous gots?"

If you want to give Tideus a Healing Potion or a Greater Healing Potion (and you haven't already), turn to **99**. If you want to give Tideus a Potion of Might (and haven't already), turn to **114**. If you've given him everything you can, turn to **129**.

325

You head for the old workshop, suspecting that maybe this fallen object came from the Nimbus explosion. It takes you a while to find it, but when you do there's a small crowd gathered nearby. The object looks like a larger metal boulder. A Goblin is trying to attach some kind of device to it. The device has a charged storm crystal inside it.

You ask a bystander what's going on.

"It's technomancy, but nothing like anyone's seen before," they explain. "Nix is going to give it a charge up and see what happens. It has already half-destroyed his workshop, so he's keen to get rid of it."

Will you:

Tell Nix that this isn't a good idea?	Turn to **19**.
Let Nix charge the metal boulder and see what happens?	Turn to **250**.

The mist begins to undulate as the hissing creature comes closer

326

Tideus and the Goblin War Golem continue their battle.

If you and Tideus are the first to win two of the next three Attack Rounds, turn to **388**. If the Goblin War Golem is the first to win two of the next three Attack Rounds, turn to **167**.

327

You decide to confront whatever lurks in the mist. As you get closer, the mist begins to undulate as the hissing creature comes closer. It rises out of the fog, lightning rolling off its long, scaly body. It's a Lightning Serpent, a rare and extremely dangerous beast.

And now you're going to have to deal with it.

LIGHTNING SERPENT   *SKILL 9*   *STAMINA 9*

If the Lightning Serpent makes a successful strike, roll one die; if you roll 4 to 6, it does double damage, as forked lightning blasts from its mouth. If you hit it, using a metal weapon, roll one die, and if you roll 5 or 6 you suffer 2 *STAMINA* points of damage too, as you are electrocuted!

If you win, turn to **95**.

328

You head out towards Altos's Great Waterfall. It is a source of water so pure that many Pangarians believe it holds healing properties. Every summer they come to bathe in the azure-blue pool at the foot of the waterfall in order to cure all their ills.

You climb closer until you find yourself on a rocky outcropping overlooking the pool. The water looks deep and strangely dark. You feel hot and bothered. You've been working hard at your investigations. A nice cool dip in these waters could be just what you need.

If you want to take a swim in the lake, turn to **291**. If you want to walk along the bank to get closer to the Great Waterfall, turn to **75**. If you want to go back and head for the Watchhouse instead, if you haven't been there already, turn to **40**.

329

You tell her that the authorities are working on a solution and that she shouldn't worry. You're sure Nimbus will be back in Pangaria soon. Maude gives you the hard stare, weighing up what you said. Turn to **364**.

330

You feel you've interrogated the Officers enough. You tell them to find somewhere safe to hide out while you continue your search. You keep your weapon drawn and head down the passageway. The air is already starting to smell a little fetid. Turn to **390**.

331

"I wouldn't if I were you, Officer. Not until the storms pass. But if you're hell-bent on reaching it, I'd say that you'd have to take one of our bathyspheres. That means going to see Matix. You can usually find her either at the main bathysphere shed at the east dock, or her home near the north flyer port."

If you have the Incus ledger page from Cirrus and want to ask them about it, turn to **308**. To look for Matix at the east dock, turn to **242**. To head for Matix's home in northern Incus, turn to **161**.

332

The sword hits the creature's wing. It drops what it was carrying and prepares to fight you.

WINGED GREMLIN   *SKILL 5*   *STAMINA 4*

If you win, turn to **122**.

333

You don't want to take any unnecessary risks with the *Barnacle*. Keeping one eye on the creature, you carefully reverse out of the passage.

To take the right fork, if you haven't already, turn to **101**. To head for the large dim shape, turn to **191**.

334

Tideus crashes to the floor, the Goblin War Golem's axe fatally imbedded in his skull. You hit the ground hard and roll for a few feet. You see the Goblin War Golem lifting one of its giant metal feet. You're too injured to move. You see the foot descend. Closer and closer. Then all goes black.

Your adventure is over.

335

You head for the Watchhouse door. You're just about to step through when *whoosh, whoosh, whoosh* – vine tendrils shoot across in front of you, blocking your exit. A bunch of grapes explodes, showering you with an acidic goo. (Lose 2 *STAMINA* points.)

The rest of the vines start to creep across the ground towards you.

If you want to use a Calming Potion on the plant, turn to **223**. If not, you are going to need to fight the vines if you want to get out of here alive.

GRAPES OF WRATH   *SKILL 7*   *STAMINA 8*

If you win, turn to **32**.

336

You continue your journey across the market, this time being more wary about who, or what, might be following you. You've not been travelling for long when a young Goblin comes running up to you with an anxious look on his face.

"I heard you were looking for me?" he pants, struggling to catch his breath.

This is definitely no Stormborn, so it must be Hazi.

"Do you have any news about him? Did he send you?"

Confused, you ask who he's referring to.

"Vizigg the Elder Technomancer, of course! You mean he hasn't sent word?"

You shake your head and explain that you're investigating what happened on Nimbus and were told you should speak to him.

Hazi sinks down on a crate, looking miserable. "I used to be an apprentice of his before he retired. He always comes here to have breakfast, but today he missed it, with no explanation. If you're heading to Asperitas, do you think you could check his house? I don't have enough coin for the flyer ride."

You assure him that you will.

"Thank you, Officer," says Hazi, looking a little more relieved.

You ask him whether he has any idea what might have happened on Nimbus.

"I've not worked there for a few years, but I still can't understand what could have caused the crash. Nimbus, like all our islands, is held up by large storm crystals. Unlike the crystals in your hovers, the island crystals are strong enough to hold their energy perpetually. If the crystals failed, then something caused that to happen. I fear it was no accident."

Add the codeword **Hazi** to your Adventure Sheet.

If you have the storm crystal shard from Cirrus, turn to **282**. If you don't have the Storm crystal shard from Cirrus, turn to **185**.

337

You are just about to set off into Incus, when a cloaked figure runs up and presses a small package into your hand. "Galen says thank you," the figure hisses, before running off.

You carefully open the package. It contains 2 Gold Pieces and a Potion of Proficiency. Seems like Galen kept his word to help you. (Add these items to your Adventure Sheet. When you drink the potion, you may ignore any penalties you suffer from using your weapon of choice and add 2 points to your Attack Strength for the duration of one battle only.) Turn to **90**.

338

You ask Vizigg about the warded Great Hall.

"After what went on, I couldn't let what might still be alive in there get out. So, I warded it whilst I worked on a solution. The ward will only last as long as I do, and my strength is fading fast."

If you want to ask him why the Nimbus crashed, and haven't already, turn to **82**. If you want to ask what Vizigg is doing with the broken storm crystals, and haven't already, turn to **59**. If you want to ask what's happened to him, and you haven't done so already, turn to **11**. If you are done asking him questions, turn to **170**.

339

You attempt to track the flying eye from below the on the streets of Asperitas. You manage to follow it surreptitiously to a cluster of houses on the outskirts of the residential area. Turn to **38**.

340

You rummage in your pack until you find something which might act as a glue. You hand it over to Grax. (Cross it off your Adventure Sheet.)

"Perfect!" he says, delighted. "Give me a few minutes and I'll have her ready for you. I only have Incus on my licenced route, so if you want to go to Asperitas, you'll have to go to the north end of Incus and pick up the Goblin flyer from there. As for Altos or Cumulus, you'll have to use your hovers. Just tell me where you'd like to go."

If you want to charge up your hovers for 1 Gold Piece and fly to Altos or Cumulus, turn to **80**.

If you'd like to take the flyer to Incus, the fishing island, turn to **8**. (If you have Silas with you, he will stay on Cirrus and you will lose your attack and damage bonuses. Adjust this on your Adventure Sheet.)

341

You select *Denizens of the Deep: Aquatic Beasts and How to Kill Them* from the shelf. Water starts to pour from the pages and pool on the floor. From the pool rises a large Sea Troll. Confused, angry, and putting the blame for its sudden predicament squarely on you, it attacks.

SEA TROLL   SKILL 8   STAMINA 9

If you win, turn to **263**.

342

You decide to visit Altos, the water island. Daxa charges up your hovers and, with a running jump, you take off into the air, leaving the markets of Cumulus behind you.

(If you have Dav with you, he will stay on Cumulus and you will lose your attack and damage bonuses. Adjust this on your Adventure Sheet.) Turn to **103**.

343

You decide to stand your ground as a winged creature shakes the ash off itself, and you realize that it's a Winged Gremlin; a particularly nasty little creature. It sees you and flies towards you *screeching* wildly.

WINGED GREMLIN   *SKILL 5*   *STAMINA 4*

If you win, turn to **122**.

This fearful creature has the head and lifeless black eyes of a shark

344

You take the *Barnacle* down the right-hand passage which is still completely flooded. There are fewer bodies here, but then you realize that the ones that are still around are horribly savaged and have been torn to shreds. You urge the *Barnacle* ahead with caution.

Suddenly there's a loud *CLANG!* and the bathysphere is sent spinning through the water.

Thinking that you may have hit something, you steady the craft before turning around to see that something has hit you instead: the trident of an angry Shark-Kin. (Deduct 2 points from the bathysphere's *STAMINA* score.) This fearful creature has the head and lifeless black eyes of a shark, with a dorsal fin in its back, but humanoid legs and savage claw-like hands.

SHARK-KIN   *SKILL 9*   *STAMINA 9*

If the Shark-Kin gets a successful strike then he will send the bathysphere spinning off with a swish of his Trident; for the next Attack Round you must reduce your Attack Strength by 1 point, due to the disorientation you are feeling. If you win, turn to **365**.

345

The name Boreas is familiar to you. You remember Methedus telling you that he was the Stormborn who made the storm crystal that landed in Cirrus, and that he also felt his presence in Nimbus when it fell. Perhaps Boreas has been making storm crystals for whatever Krazic has been working on in secret.

You exit the room and look at the chaos in the house, and the deep grooves on the walls. Now you know how deeply a Stormborn was involved, you can't help but think that maybe Boreas was behind the destruction that's wreaked this havoc. You suspect foul play is at work, although there are no bodies to prove that. But from what that diary entry said, there may be even worse to come for Pangaria.

There's nothing left to do but press on.

To leave and go towards Matix's home, turn to **161**. To leave and head to the east dock and the bathysphere workshop, turn to **74**.

346

"Would you look at that?" he grumbles, gesturing to his damaged balloon when he sees you approach. "I was just having a spot of lunch and minding my own business, when I hears a huge bang and a great big rock hits the old girl and gives her a gaping big hole in her side! And I dropped my best pie over the edge of the island!"

He sadly strokes the deflated balloon. "There, there, old girl," he murmurs gently. "Soon as Grax finds you a patch and some glue, we'll get you up and floating about again."

You ask if you can be of any help.

"Thank you, Officer," says Grax, looking a little more cheerful. "If you happen upon something I can fashion into a patch, that would help. Or if you've got some coin, you can charge up the crystal in those hovers of yours. They won't take you to the furthest islands, but they should get you to Altos or Cumulus. Usually you'd be able to use the Sky Bridge to Cumulus, but it's been closed, due to some unusual energies on the Cumulus side, so your hovers or my flyer are your best bet for now.

If you have a cabbage leaf or a silk cloth, turn to **200**. If not, you have no choice but to pay to charge up your hovers – turn to **80**. If you do not have any Gold Pieces, you can continue no further and your adventure is over.

347

You're back in the antechamber.

If you have the codeword **Nimbi** on your Adventure Sheet, turn to **92**.

If not, and you want to continue to the steps ahead, and haven't done so already, turn to **252**. If you want to leave the Citadel, turn to **256**.

You stand up to see Galen Hillcroft, a fellow Altos Sky Watch recruit, looking confused and holding a burning log from the fire.

"It's you!" Galen exclaims. "But how did you get out of the Cita—"

He stops himself. You feel the anger rising within you. Did he know what was going to happen? Before he can react, you pin him against the wall, with your sword at his neck, and demand he tells you what he knows.

"Nothing, I swear, I just got a message saying not to go to the meeting at the Citadel on Nimbus this morning. It didn't say why. When I saw what happened, I decided to hide out here. I think I dozed off for a minute or two."

You ask him who sent the message. He's reluctant to answer, and although you hate to threaten a fellow Sky Watch Officer, this is not a time for secrets. You push your sword against his throat.

"Easy, easy, you know me. I wouldn't do something like this, would I?"

He's right, you're having a hard time believing Galen is responsible for bringing down Nimbus; he's far too lazy for a start. You relax your grip and lower your sword.

Galen seizes the opportunity and shoves you back hard. By the time you regain your balance, he has grabbed a sword of his own.

"Only one of us is getting out of this Watchhouse alive.

And I'm telling you now, pal, it's gonna be me."

GALEN HILLCROFT   *SKILL 7*   *STAMINA 7*

If you manage to reduce your opponent's *STAMINA* score to 3 points or fewer, turn to **374** at once.

349

You explain that you must find the Nimbus first, but once you have done, you'll send help for him. The fisherman doesn't look very convinced and stuffs the wool tufts back in his ears. (Lose 1 *LUCK* point.)

You continue deeper into the storm. Turn to **93**.

350

As you climb the wooden stairs you can hear a *rhythmic metallic grating* sound. You reach the upper room and see two beds. They are both unmade and unoccupied. Near the end of the room is a hatch connected to a large cage in which you can see three of the metal Eye-Spy creatures, sitting on perches like birds. They seem to be sleeping, making small snoring noises, as they dream of ... whatever it is that large metal eyeballs dream of.

Nearby is a large crystal ball and surrounding it are pages and pages of notes and sketches.

You look harder at the sleeping Eye-Spies and see that there are tiny storm crystals inside them. You can also see that the perch is made of metal and wires, connected to a box-like device with a prominent lever. The Eye-Spies are perching on little nests which you realize must be charging the crystals.

If you have the codeword **Eye-Spy** on your Adventure Sheet, turn to **29**. If you do not have the codeword on your Adventure Sheet, turn to **315**.

351

You continue through the main market. A few market-goers nervously ask you what's going on and if they are safe. You tell them that you're investigating matters and they should carefully continue their business as normal until they receive further information. Privately you have no idea what that information is going to be, or if anyone is safe, but there's no sense in creating more panic.

You're walking along, taking in the sights, sounds and smells at the market, when you feel a light tugging at your belt. You turn to see a creature that looks like a Cockroach the size of a dog skittering off with your Coin Bag in its mouth.

If your Coin Bag is empty, turn to **336**. If your Coin Bag still has some money in it, turn to **355**.

352

You decide to head to the bell tower. After all, you told Hazi you would check on Elder Techromancer Vizigg. It takes a bit of time to reach the tower, but thankfully there are no more ambushes.

You clang the brass bell by the door, but there's no answer. Either Vizigg's not at home, or something's happened to him. You test the door and discover its locked. It looks strong. You square up to it.

Test Your Stamina, subtracting 2 from the dice roll if you have an axe or club-like weapon with you. If you pass the test, turn to **234**. If you fail the test, turn to **294**.

353

With a last roar of thunder the Stormkin disintegrates into thin air.

The Cloudkin farmer is your friend Nemi, and she throws her arms around you. "I was so worried about you," she cries. "I heard that something terrible had happened on Nimbus, but then the Cloudkin went stormy and all hell broke loose. Most of the other workers fled, but I wasn't going to give up my farm that easily!"

You tell Nemi that you are investigating what happened on Nimbus, as the last member of the Sky Watch still in Pangaria.

"Hmm," says Nemi thoughtfully. "You might not be the last one; I went by the Watchhouse just before the explosion and I heard snoring coming from inside."

Seems that someone else didn't make the meeting. That sounds like something you should check out.

"Right, well, the farm is safe for now. How about you keep the Cloudkin Staff and I come with you on your travels? Well, at least on Altos. I can back you up in a fight and I want to find out what's happened to Flapps, my best Canidor. Most of the Canidors scattered when the explosion happened and haven't been seen since. I'm really worried about him. Hopefully, he's in hiding; he always liked the area up by the Great Waterfall. And here, you'd better take this." She passes you a Healing Potion. (This will restore up to 4 *STAMINA* points when drunk.)

With Nemi by your side you can add 2 points when calculating your Attack Strength, you may increase any damage you cause by 1 point, and you may reduce any damage you suffer in battle by 1 point. (Make a note of this on your Adventure Sheet.)

(If you choose to use the wooden Cloudkin staff in battle, you must reduce your Attack Strength by 1 point against opponents that aren't Cloudkin, as it is more cumbersome to use than your Short Sword. For now, add the staff to your Adventure Sheet.)

Now you just have to decide where you and Nemi will go next. If you want to go towards the Altos Watchhouse, turn to **40**. If you want to go towards the Great Waterfall, turn to **328**.

354

You jump out of the way as part of the ceiling collapses directly above you, but you're not quite fast enough and some of the broken floorboards hit you on their way down. (Lose 3 *STAMINA* points and 1 *SKILL* point.)

Once you've recovered, you notice the strange marks on the walls of the house, for the first time. They look like ridges or large scratches. Something very strange has happened here.

If you have the storm crystal shard from Cirrus, turn to **235**. If not, turn to **279**.

355

Remove all the Gold Pieces from the Gold Box on your Adventure Sheet.

If Dav is with you, turn to **141**. If Dav is not with you, turn to **307**.

356

You ask the Officer about what happened to his friend.

"Hey! I ain't dead, you can still talk to me!" says the injured Officer grumpily, and introduces himself as Bal.

"I got a leg full of spines from one of those bouncing beasties. You don't have a healing potion on you, do you?"

If you have a Healing Potion on you and want to give it to Bal, turn to **107**. If you want to ask them what happened to the Nimbus, turn to **77**. If you want to ask if there are any other survivors, turn to **197**. If you've asked them everything you want to, turn to **330**.

357

You stare at the thing making the *buzzing* noise. It looks like a metal eye, about the size of a grapefruit, and instead of an iris, you realize that the metal contraption has a large lens. It is held up by small wings, reminiscent of your hovers. The eye zips around, blinking at you. It's unnerving and you can't shake the feeling that you're being spied on. Suddenly it flies off.

You decide to follow it.

Roll one die. If you roll a 1 or 2, turn to **76**. If you roll 3 or 4, turn to **142**. If you roll a 5 or 6, turn to **339**.

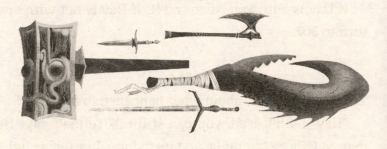

358

The Wheelies crash to the floor, rock back and forth for a bit, and then lie still. You wonder what they were guarding.

The ground floor of the house is so full of hoarded

objects that it's hard to see what might be useful to your investigation. You discern that the house has at least two messy occupants. Your eye is drawn to a leather bag hanging off a hook. The Goblin was in such a hurry to get away from you that he must've forgotten it. The name inscribed on the bag reads "Paxlo".

You search Paxlo's bag and find a Potion of fire oil, a piece of dried fruit, and 2 Gold Pieces. This will be some compensation for the assault you suffered at the hands of the Wheelies. Add these to your Adventure Sheet.

(The fire oil can be used to light fires but it can also be used against an opponent at the start of an Attack Round and will automatically cause your enemy 3 *STAMINA* points of damage. The Dried Fruit will restore up to 3 *STAMINA* points, when eaten.)

If you want to explore the upper floor of the house, turn to **350**. If you want to leave the property, turn to **149**.

359

You struggle against whatever is restraining you, kicking out with both feet. Your attacker clearly wasn't ready for such a fight and lets you go. You surface quickly and swim for the shore. Turn to **314**.

360

You successfully make the jump and easily pull yourself up into the room above. Turn to **313**.

361

The Goblin flyer bobs up and down on the breeze as you approach. However, its pilot sits nearby, holding his head in his hands and *moaning* gently. You recognize the pilot as a Goblin named Kritch and ask him what's the matter.

"Bit of rubble hit me upside the head," says Kritch. "I ain't flying nowhere until I get a bit of healing. But if you're looking to charge your hovers, then the machine is over there."

If you want to give him a cabbage leaf or some healing honey (if you have either), turn to **20**. If you want to charge your hovers for 1 Gold Piece, turn to **96**. If you do not have any Gold Pieces, you can continue no further and your adventure is over.

362

You're not quite skilful enough at piloting the craft and large sections of rock dent the *Barnacle*'s roof. (The craft loses 2 *STAMINA* points. Adjust this on your Adventure Sheet.) The vibrations cease, as do the falling rocks. The tunnel ahead is now blocked, so there's nothing for it but to go back the way you came and explore elsewhere.

To take the right fork, if you haven't already, turn to **101**. To head for the large dim shape, turn to **191**.

363

Your sword skewers the creature, killing it stone dead. It drops what it was carrying and collapses in a heap. Turn to **122**.

364

"Well, you'll be needing a bit of help then," says Maude, going into her little cottage and coming out with a War-Hammer and a Healing Potion. "Use them well and wisely. I'll be ordering a few more Cloudkin from Altos just in case these trees start firing up again."

(If you use Maude's War-Hammer, you may add 1 point to any damage you cause an opponent, but must reduce your Attack Strength by 1 point, due to its weight. The Healing Potion will restore up to 4 *STAMINA* points when drunk. Record the War-Hammer and the Healing Potion in the Equipment box on your Adventure Sheet.)

If you now want to investigate the plume of blue-green smoke, turn to **137**. If you want to head north, turn to **255**.

365

The Shark-Kin's lifeless body floats away from you, but his trident looks in good condition. You use the *Barnacle*'s suction pipe to retrieve it. (Make a note of the trident on your Adventure Sheet. If you use the trident in battle, you must reduce your Attack Strength by 1 point, but on a successful strike roll one die; if you roll 4 to 6, the weapon does 3 *STAMINA* points damage rather than the usual 2.)

You move the *Barnacle* further down the corridor. There is a blocked door ahead of you, but also some steps leading up to a door on a higher level.

To head back to the antechamber, turn to **347**. To bring the bathysphere to the steps, climb out, and make your way up to the higher door, turn to **280**.

366

You can't quite grasp the paper and your exasperated signing only blows it further under the skirting board out of reach. You tell yourself that it probably wasn't important anyway.

There's nothing left to do here, so you decide to press on with your investigation.

If you want to leave and go towards Matix's home, turn to **161**. If you want to head to the east dock and the bathysphere workshop, turn to **74**.

367

Once the creatures are slain, you retrieve your Coin Bag. A glittering from inside the pipe draws your eye. Reaching your hand carefully inside, you find 2 Gold Pieces. (Add these to the Gold Box on your Adventure Sheet.) Turn to **336**.

368

The beast lies dead at your feet. You find a longsword, lying amongst the rocks and dirt of the cave.

(Record the longsword on your Adventure Sheet. If you use the longsword in battle, you may increase your Attack Strength by 1 point.)

If you want to investigate the Goblin flyer, turn to **361**. If you haven't been to the Watchhouse and want to go there now, turn to **40**.

369

You're just reaching for the large iron latch on the Great Hall door when a surge of energy pushes you back. (Lose 1 *STAMINA* point.) There seems to be a ward around the door, preventing anyone from entering. You wonder who is left inside the Citadel with the ability to conjure such a ward. For now, this way is inaccessible. You weigh up your other options.

If you want to venture down the half-flooded hallway, turn to **127**. If you want to see what might be left in the kitchens, turn to **9**.

"He's coming! He's coming! Oh, you're in trouble now!"

You realize now that the great metal face isn't human. It's a giant metal Goblin. It seems that although they are adept at technomancy, they're not particularly imaginative.

The small Goblin face screeches down from the large metal one: "Get me out of here! Don't you know who I am?"

It's Krazic, the Chief Engineer. Without the power of the storm crystal, he's trapped inside the Golem. In fact, you realize when you look at the joints of the metal beast that you can see eyes blinking back. There are other Goblins inside the Golem, all now prisoners.

You shout back up that you know what he did, and he will be brought to justice when Nimbus reaches Pangaria. This enrages Krazic. "No! We Goblins have been constrained too long by Pangaria's so-called justice, by her rules. Our skills should not be hidden away. They should be shown to the world!"

Given there's nothing Krazic can do to hurt you, his furious outbursts from the prison of his own creation are almost comical.

That feeling quickly passes when you feel a wind spring up; odd, considering where you are and the fact that the island is still not out of the water yet. The wind becomes more intense. Krazic yells excitedly, "He's coming! He's coming! Oh, you're in trouble now!"

You pull back behind a pile of rubble with Malia as an

ethereal figure appears in the middle of the storm. It's Boreas the Stormborn and he's extremely angry.

He conjures a whirlwind, which draws lumps of rubble towards him, and then flings the deadly mess in your direction.

Test Your Skill. If you are Successful, turn to **165**. If you are Unsuccessful, turn to **128**.

371

You wonder briefly why the chest has been left unopened, but when you lift the lid, you get your answer. The chest bites down on your hand (lose 2 *STAMINA* points and 1 *SKILL* point) and starts to bark and growl at you. It snaps its lid aggressively.

If you have a Calming Potion and want to use it now, cross it off your Adventure Sheet and turn to **130**. If not, you are going to have to fight the Chest Creature.

CHEST CREATURE   SKILL 5   STAMINA 6

If you win, turn to **130**.

372

You tell Yurik that you know he's involved.

"You're lying, Officer, because I ain't! *I ain't!* Was it Pox? Or Paxlo? Did they say something?

If you want to ask Yurik who Pox and Paxlo are, turn

to **221**. If you want to tell Yurik that it was Pox who said something, turn to **53**.

373

With a shudder, the Giant Scorpion curls up and dies. You cut off its stinger and carefully store it in your bag. (Add the stinger to your Equipment List. It can be used to coat your weapon with poison for one battle only; however, your weapon will cause 1 extra point of damage with every successful hit for the duration of that battle.)

Now you can investigate the *clicking* noise you heard before the creature appeared. You test the bookcase and find that part of it now swings back, revealing a set of wooden stairs spirally downwards.

Taking care, you head down. Turn to **292**.

374

You raise your sword to dispense the killing blow.

"No, no, please, please," he begs. "Don't do this. If you let me live, I won't cause any trouble and I'll find a way to help you, I swear!"

If you decide to let him live, turn to **81**. If you think that he must die, turn to **260**.

375

You hand the requested object to Matix and she holds it almost reverentially. "Wow, that is one of the best I've ever seen. This will definitely work!"

If you have a Thingie, and haven't already given it to Matix, you can do so now by turning to **125**. If you have now given Matix everything she requested, turn to **187**. If you haven't collected all of the items Matix needs yet, you will need to get your hovers charged up again – turn to **396**.

376

On the way to the shed you pass by an empty wooden frame. A crow perches on it, preening itself. It *caws* angrily and takes flight when a large cabbage is hurled at it. A straw-filled figure lumbers out from behind the shed. It's the frame's original occupant, an enraged Scarecrow. It plucks a couple of heavy-looking cabbages and aims them at your head.

SCARECROW   SKILL 6   STAMINA 5

If you win, turn to **271**.

377

You guide the *Barnacle* down the flooded main corridor. Every now and then you see bodies float past. You can't let yourself look in case you recognize anyone; that would be too much to handle right now and you have a job to do.

The water level starts to drop, and you realize you're entering a large air bubble. The *Barnacle* floats halfway out of the water for a little while before you enter an antechamber and see some more steps and a fully flooded tunnel to your right.

To pull the *Barnacle* up next to the steps, turn to **252**. To explore the flooded right-hand corridor, turn to **344**.

378

You make sure Halleck is comfortable and tell him you're going to continue searching the Citadel.

"Good work, Officer!" he says, saluting you.

You leave the kitchen via the main door.

If you have the codeword **Nimbi** on your Adventure Sheet, turn to **92**. If not, turn to **390**.

379

You reach the nearest charging station. It requires 1 Gold Piece to use.

If you have no gold, then you can return to the previous section and continue exploring Asperitas until you find some.

If you have explored all you can and still have no gold, then your adventure is over.

To fly to Matix on Incus deduct 1 Gold Piece from your Adventure Sheet and turn to **226**.

380

You remove the corrosive grapes carefully from their pouch. Using your staff, you crush them against the lock of the Watchhouse door. The juice begins to eat away at the metal, making a satisfying *hissing* sound. Soon the lock breaks and you head inside to find the source of the snoring. Turn to **306**.

381

You ram the door. It gives, but doesn't break. (Lose 2 *STAMINA* points, as you bruise your shoulder in trying to force your way in.)

If you want to try ramming the door a second time, turn to **229**. If you think you would be better off leaving the property, turn to **149**.

382

You manage to roll out of the way as the Giant metal foot crashes down beside you. You lash out with your weapon.

(Deduct 2 *STAMINA* points from the War Golem.) Turn to **100**.

383

Your short sword skewers the creature perfectly. It *screeches*, shakes and goes limp. You retrieve your Coin Bag and the weapon, cleaning it thoroughly.

A glittering from inside the pipe draws your eye. Reaching inside you find 2 Gold Pieces. (Add these to the Gold Box on your Adventure Sheet, along with the original number of Gold Pieces you had when the bug stole your Coin Bag.) Turn to **336**.

384

You grudgingly give 1 Gold Piece to Matix and ask her to charge up your hovers so you can fly to Asperitas.

"Sure thing! Put your storm crystal in the slot and I'll fill her up!"

Once your storm crystal is fully charged, Matix gives some final instructions.

"Now, once you find a Thingie, and either a Doobry or a Wotsit, bring them back to me here. There should be a couple of places you can charge your hovers on the other islands."

You strap on the hovers and take off for Asperitas, the island of technomancy. Turn to **270**.

385

As the corpse of the Great White Squark sinks into the depths, you manage to activate the *Barnacle*'s suction tube on the right pincer and capture yourself a piece of fresh calamari. (Add this to your Provisions list. It will restore up to 3 *STAMINA* when eaten.)

You feel the water vibrate around you. You brace yourself, but nothing appears, and eventually the vibrations cease.

You survey the depths. There's a large dim shape in the distance. It could be a rock formation, or it could be the sunken Nimbus. There are also some interesting-looking caves below you which could be worth investigating.

If you want to head towards the caves, turn to **85**. To continue towards the large dim shape, turn to **191**.

386

It's not an easy task, and you strain your back in the process, but you eventually pull the last of the debris from Captain Halleck. (Lose 1 *STAMINA* point and 1 *SKILL* point.)

Halleck's legs are so badly damaged that he can hardly walk, so you find him a more comfortable place to rest. Turn to **148**.

387

The boot is well-aimed and strikes the flying eye. Something metal falls off the side of it. The contraption emits a high-pitched noise, before flying away up the Watchhouse chimney.

You examine what fell off it. It's a Strange Metal Object. (Add this to your Equipment List.)

You're unharmed but can't shake the feeling that you're being watched. However, there's no time to dwell on such things right now – you need to get moving!

(Write the codeword **Eye-Spy** on your Adventure Sheet.)

Choosing something you've not already tried, will you:

Search your chest?	Turn to **217**.
See what Silas found earlier?	Turn to **134**.
Leave the Watchhouse?	Turn to **335**.

388

The battle is almost yours; you can feel it. You can see that the Goblins controlling the Golem's legs are weakening. You leap off Tideus's shoulder and run circles around the construct's legs, slashing at them with your weapon.

Test Your Stamina. If you are Successful, turn to **300**. If you are Unsuccessful, turn to **192**.

389

You pull the lever. There's a *whirring* and a *thrumming*, then all three Eye-Spies emit a *piercing shriek* and explode, showering you in bits of metal and wire.

(Roll one die and divide the result by 2, rounding halves up; deduct this many *STAMINA* points.)

You pick up an interesting-looking part from the device, which seems to be undamaged. It looks like it could be a Wotsit. (Add the Wotsit to your Adventure Sheet.)

If you haven't explored the ground floor yet, and want to, turn to **182**. If you want to leave the property, turn to **149**.

Alternatively, you can go to the nearest storm crystal charging station. If you decide to do this, make a note of this section number, as you will be able to return directly to this location if you decide to revisit Asperitas, and then turn to **379**.

390

You arrive in an open area. It's the Nimbiferous Chamber, one of the central locations in the Citadel. Ahead is a large door that leads to the Great Hall.

You peer down the hallway to the right. It is partially collapsed and flooded, but you think you should be able to

391

wade through. You're pretty sure that the hallway to the left leads to the Citadel kitchens. Your stomach rumbles at the thought of food.

(Add the codeword **Nimbi** to your Adventure Sheet.)

If you want to venture down the half-flooded hallway, and you haven't done so before, turn to **127**. If your stomach has taken control and you want to see what's left in the kitchens, turn to **9**. If you want to open the door to the Great Hall, turn to **369**.

391

A small pair of webbed, clawed hands appear on the edge of the puddle and a Mudclaw hops out of it. You can tell by the look on Boreas's face that he had expected something a lot more impressive, or at least a pack of Mudclaws. This is barely a fight, but you'd better engage quickly, in case more of them appear.

MUDCLAW   SKILL 5   STAMINA 4

If you win, turn to **392**.

You feel your heart sink and your blood run cold

As you lay the killing blow, Boreas looks at you with eyes of wrath.

"Clearly there is only one last thing I need to do," he says in a tone that chills you.

And with that the Stormborn dives into the chest of the Golem, fusing himself with the remains of the fractured crystal. His energy flows through the creation as he turns himself into a living storm crystal.

You feel your heart sink and your blood run cold as the Goblin War Golem lumbers into life, pulling itself from the rubble. You know that you can't fight it on your own. You're going to have to call in a favour.

Whilst the Golem is righting itself, you quickly get Malia to safety and tell her to head for the kitchens.

You hate to wake up a sleeping Sea Giant a second time, but it's urgent. You press the conch shell to your lips and blow.

A low mournful sound echoes around the Citadel. In the distance you hear *thumping*, and *crashing*, and then there is a knocking sound at the Great Hall door. It takes you a moment to realize that it's a *kicking* sound. You run to open the door, but Tideus, not one to be tied down by convention, decides to crash through the wall next to it instead.

He eyes up the Golem. "Ho! Ho! Ho! A nice big fight for Tideus? Hooman, you is spoiling Tideus! Just wish Tideus was at full strength."

TIDEUS   SKILL 9   STAMINA 10

Make a note of the stats that Tideus currently has on your Adventure Sheet. It seems he's still not completely recovered from the last battle with you. Then you remember that many potions are unaffected by the size of the creature consuming them and realize you might have a few things that could give Tideus a boost for the fight ahead.

If you want to give Tideus a Healing Potion or a Greater Healing Potion, then turn to **99**. If you want to give Tideus a Potion of Might, turn to **114**. If you want to give Tideus a Potion of Power, turn to **324**.

If you have none of these potions, or do not want to give any of them to the Sea Giant, turn to **129**.

393

You draw close to the *Barracuda*. The gash in its side is sizeable and it makes you remember just how vulnerable you are in your little spherical craft. You get a shock when a dead, bloated face floats into view, half eaten by crabs. It's the *Barracuda*'s former pilot. Horrified, you knock the crabs off the body with the *Barnacle*'s pincers. You're sure they'll probably return, but you can't watch them eating the poor man's flesh.

You spot some waterproof firesticks and a Greater Healing Potion floating in the wreckage and manage to gather them with your suction pipe. (Add them to your Adventure Sheet. The potion will restore up to 5 *STAMINA* points when drunk.)

Now there's nothing for it but to make your way to the Citadel. Turn to **290**.

394

You patrol the seabed for some time but find nothing that can help you in your quest, so you head back to the Citadel's antechamber. However, the air in the bathysphere is starting to run out and you begin to feel light-headed. (Reduce your *SKILL* score by 1 point.) Turn to **347**.

395

Silas pulls your arm again and whispers, "Hey! Hey! Do you hear that?"

There's a strange *buzzing* sound on the edge of hearing, like the rapid flapping of tiny wings.

"There!" says Silas, pointing to the corner of the Watchhouse.

You peer into the gloom and see something that looks like a metal eye. It is about the size of a grapefruit and instead of an iris, you realize that the metal contraption has a large lens. It is held up by small wings, reminiscent of your hovers.

"What is it?" says Silas worriedly, although the strange thing seems to be posing no threat, but you have no idea. The eye zips around, blinking at you and Silas.

Silas throws his boot at it.

Roll one die. If you roll a 1 or 2, turn to **297**. If you roll a 3 or 4, turn to **71**. If you roll a 5 or 6, turn to **387**.

396

You tell Matix that you still have an item to collect.

If you have at least 1 Gold Piece, you put it into her open hand and she charges up the crystal in your hovers; adjust your Adventure Sheet accordingly and turn to **270**.

If you do not have any Gold Pieces, you can continue no further and your adventure is over.

397

The globule hits your arm, gluing it to a tree. The slime is also slightly acidic and burns your skin (lose 3 *STAMINA* points).

A Giant Toad waddles out of the swamp, blocking your path. It readies itself to launch another gloopy missile in your direction. Desperation lends you the strength to pull your arm free.

To fight the creature, turn to **44**. If you have a Calming Potion and want to use it, turn to **204**.

398

You arm yourself with your weapon of choice and face the scaly beast.

SALTWATER CROCODILE   *SKILL* 8   *STAMINA* 8

When you reduce the Crocodile's *STAMINA* score to 4 points or fewer, it retreats a little, allowing you to move the fight out of the water and on to dry land. From then onwards, reduce the Crocodile's Attack Strength by 2 Points.

If you win, turn to **66**.

"Uh-oh!" says Dav in response to the ground trembling beneath your feet. "Something's on its way and it's BIG! I smell a fight coming!" He reaches into a small bag at his waist and tosses you a small bottle of purplish-coloured liquid.

"Take this. It'll give you a little extra oomph."

You see the earth bucking and cracking as something burrows through the soil towards you, sending market stalls flying.

Hands shaking, you gulp down the liquid. A warm, tingling feeling washes through your body, right down to the tips of your fingers. You feel your strength growing. (Add 3 *STAMINA* points to your total, even if this takes it above its *Initial* level, and add 1 point when calculating your Attack Strength for this fight only.)

As the feeling surges through you, a huge worm-like creature erupts from the ground. It seems to have no eyes, but it makes up for that with the number of glistening fangs it has in its huge, gaping mouth, which is heading straight for you.

"Give it hell!" yells Dav.

TUNNELLER BEAST   *SKILL 8*   *STAMINA 9*

If you win, turn to **289**.

400

The sun is starting to rise as Nimbus takes its rightful place in the centre of the Pangarian archipelago. You can hear the faint sound of cheering from the nearest islands and the Goblin flyers come out to greet you. Peace has been restored.

The rest of the world may never know how close it came to disaster and what you did to save it. But there are plenty on Pangaria who will know. Songs will be sung about you and poems written. Your deeds will not be forgotten.

But with Commander Matias Talliman still on the loose somewhere in Khul, his head full of Pangaria's technomancy secrets, Captain Halleck tasks you with journeying there to bring the rogue to justice.

This adventure might be over, but there will be many more to come . . .

HOW TO FIGHT
THE CREATURES OF
PANGARIA

Before embarking on your adventure, you must first determine your own strengths and weaknesses. Use dice to determine your initial scores. On pages 278–279 there is an *Adventure Sheet* which you may use to record details of an adventure. On it you will find boxes for recording your *SKILL*, *STAMINA* and *LUCK* scores.

You are advised either to record your scores on the *Adventure Sheet* in pencil or to make photocopies of the sheet for use in future adventures.

SKILL, STAMINA AND LUCK

To determine your *Initial SKILL*, *STAMINA* and *LUCK* scores:
- Roll one die. Add 6 to this number and enter this total in the *SKILL* box on the *Adventure Sheet*.
- Roll both dice. Add 12 to the number rolled and enter this total in the *STAMINA* box.
- Roll one die, add 6 to this number and enter this total in the *LUCK* box.

SKILL reflects your swordsmanship and fighting expertise; the higher the better, *STAMINA* represents your strength; the higher your *STAMINA*, the longer you will survive, *LUCK* represents how lucky a person you are. Luck – and magic – are facts of life in the fantasy world you are about to explore.

SKILL, *STAMINA* and *LUCK* scores change constantly during an adventure, so keep an eraser handy. You must keep an accurate record of these scores. But never rub out your *Initial* scores. Although you may receive additional *SKILL*, *STAMINA* and *LUCK* points, these totals may never exceed your *Initial* scores, except on very rare occasions, when instructed on a particular page.

BATTLES

You will often come across pages in the book which instruct you to fight a creature of some sort. An option to flee may be given, but if not – or if you choose to attack the creature anyway – you must resolve the battle as described below.

First record the creature's *SKILL* and *STAMINA* scores in the first vacant Monster Encounter Box on your *Adventure Sheet*. The scores for each creature are given in the book each time you have an encounter.

The sequence of combat is then:

1. Roll both dice once for the creature. Add its *SKILL* score. This total is the creature's Attack Strength.

2. Roll both dice once for yourself. Add the number rolled to your current *SKILL* score. This total is your Attack Strength.

3. If your Attack Strength is higher than that of the creature, you have wounded it. Proceed to step 4. If the creature's Attack Strength is higher than yours, it has wounded you. Proceed to step 5. If both Attack Strength totals are the same, you have avoided each other's blows – start the next Attack Round from step 1 above.

4. You have wounded the creature, so subtract 2 points from its *STAMINA* score. You may use your *LUCK* here to do additional damage (see over).

5. The creature has wounded you, so subtract 2 points from your own *STAMINA* score. Again, you may use *LUCK* at this stage (see over).

6. Make the appropriate adjustments to either the creature's or your own *STAMINA* scores (and your *LUCK* score if you used *LUCK* – see over).

7. Begin the next Attack Round by returning to your current *SKILL* score and repeating steps 1–6. This sequence continues until the *STAMINA* score of either you or the creature you are fighting has been reduced to zero (death).

FIGHTING MORE THAN ONE CREATURE

If you come across more than one creature in a particular encounter, the instructions on that page will tell you how to handle the battle. Sometimes you will treat them as a single monster; sometimes you will fight each one in turn.

LUCK

At various times during your adventure, either in battles or when you come across situations in which you could be either lucky or unlucky (details of these are given on the pages themselves), you may call on your *LUCK* to make the outcome more favourable. But beware! Using *LUCK* is a risky business, and if you are *un*lucky, the results could be disastrous.

The procedure for using your *LUCK* is as follows: roll two dice. If the number rolled is equal to or less than your current *LUCK* score, you have been lucky and the result will go in your favour. If the number rolled is higher than

your current *LUCK* score, you have been unlucky and you will be penalized.

This procedure is known as *Testing your Luck.* Each time

you *Test your Luck,* you must subtract one point from your current *LUCK* score. Thus you will soon realize that the more you rely on your *LUCK*, the more risky this will become.

Using Luck in Battles

On certain pages of the book you will be told to *Test your Luck* and will be told the consequences of your being lucky or unlucky. However, in battles, you always have the option of using your *LUCK* either to inflict a more serious wound on a creature you have just wounded, or to minimize the effects of a wound the creature has just inflicted on you.

If you have just wounded the creature, you may *Test your Luck* as described above. If you are Lucky, you have inflicted a severe wound and may subtract an extra 2 points from the creature's *STAMINA* score. However, if you are Unlucky, the wound was a mere graze and you must restore 1 point to the creature's *STAMINA* (i.e. instead of scoring the normal 2 points of damage, you have now scored only 1).

If the creature has just wounded you, you may *Test your Luck* to try to minimize the wound. If you are Lucky, you have managed to avoid the full damage of the blow. Restore

1 point of *STAMINA* (i.e. instead of doing 2 points of damage it has done only 1). If you are Unlucky, you have taken a more serious blow. Subtract 1 extra *STAMINA* point.

Remember that you must subtract 1 point from your *LUCK* score every time you *Test your Luck*.

MORE ABOUT YOUR ATTRIBUTES

Skill

Your *SKILL* score will not change much during your adventure. Occasionally, a paragraph may give instructions to increase or decrease your *SKILL* score A Magic Weapon may increase your *SKILL* – but remember that only one weapon can be used at a time! You cannot claim 2 *SKILL* bonuses for carrying 2 Magic Swords. Your *SKILL* score can never exceed its *Initial* value unless you are specifically instructed otherwise.

Stamina

Your *STAMINA* score will change a lot during your adventure as you fight monsters and undertake arduous tasks. As you near your goal, your *STAMINA* level may become dangerously low and battles may be particularly risky, so be careful!

Unlike other Fighting Fantasy Gamebooks, in this adventure you do not begin with any Provisions. However, during the course of the adventure, you will have opportunities to regain *STAMINA* points in various ways.

Remember also that your *STAMINA* score may never exceed its *Initial* value unless you are instructed to the contrary in a specific paragraph.

Testing your Skill and Stamina

At various times you will be told to *Test your Skill*. The procedure for Testing your Skill works as follows: roll two dice. If the number rolled is equal to or less than your current *SKILL* score, you have succeeded in your test and the result will go in your favour. If the number rolled is higher than your current *SKILL* score, you will have failed the test and will have to suffer the consequences. However, unlike Testing your Luck, do not subtract 1 point from your *SKILL* each time you Test your Skill.

You may also be told to *Test your Stamina* from time to time. To do so, roll three dice. If the total rolled is equal to or less than your current *STAMINA* score, you have been successful. However, if the total rolled is higher than your current *STAMINA* score, you have been unsuccessful. Whenever you *Test your Stamina*, do not subtract any STAMINA points, unless specifically told to do so.

Luck

Additions to your LUCK score are awarded during the adventure when you have been particularly lucky Details are given in the paragraphs of the book. Remember that, as with *SKILL* and *STAMINA*, your *LUCK* score may never exceed its *Initial* value unless you are specifically instructed otherwise.

EQUIPMENT

You start your adventure with the basic tools of your trade: a fine sword; clothes suitable for travelling; a backpack to hold any treasure you may come across; and a lantern to light your way.

ADVENTURE SHEET

SKILL
INITIAL
SKILL:

STAMINA
INITIAL
STAMINA:

LUCK
INITIAL
LUCK:

ITEMS

PROVISIONS

GOLD

WEAPONS

CODEWORDS

MONSTER ENCOUNTERS

SKILL	**SKILL**	**SKILL**
STAMINA	**STAMINA**	**STAMINA**
SKILL	**SKILL**	**SKILL**
STAMINA	**STAMINA**	**STAMINA**
SKILL	**SKILL**	**SKILL**
STAMINA	**STAMINA**	**STAMINA**
SKILL	**SKILL**	**SKILL**
STAMINA	**STAMINA**	**STAMINA**

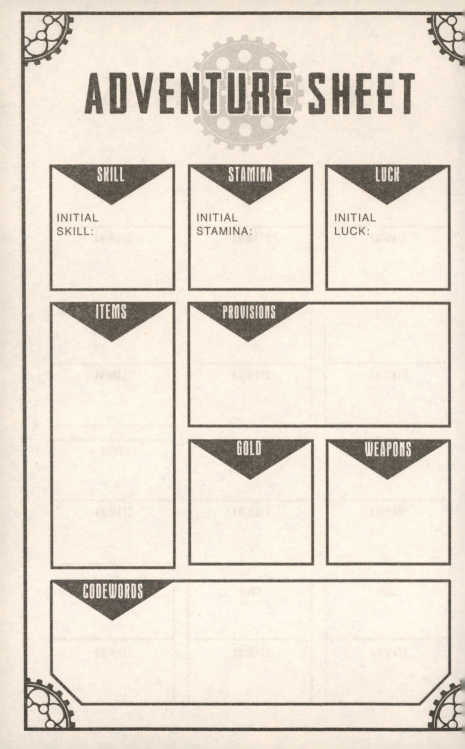

ADVENTURE SHEET

SKILL
INITIAL
SKILL:

STAMINA
INITIAL
STAMINA:

LUCK
INITIAL
LUCK:

ITEMS

PROVISIONS

GOLD

WEAPONS

CODEWORDS

MONSTER ENCOUNTERS

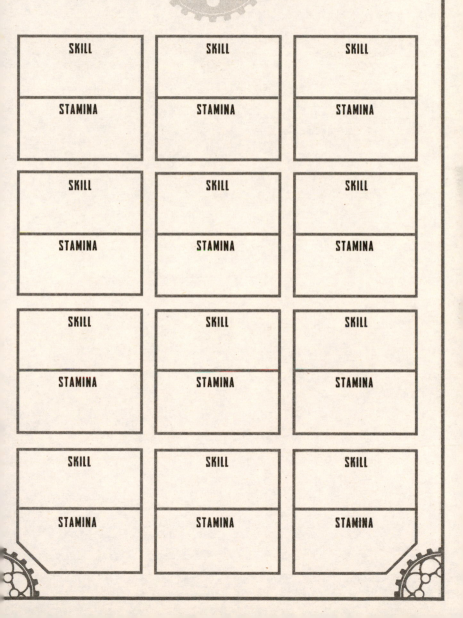

SKILL	SKILL	SKILL
STAMINA	STAMINA	STAMINA

SKILL	SKILL	SKILL
STAMINA	STAMINA	STAMINA

SKILL	SKILL	SKILL
STAMINA	STAMINA	STAMINA

SKILL	SKILL	SKILL
STAMINA	STAMINA	STAMINA

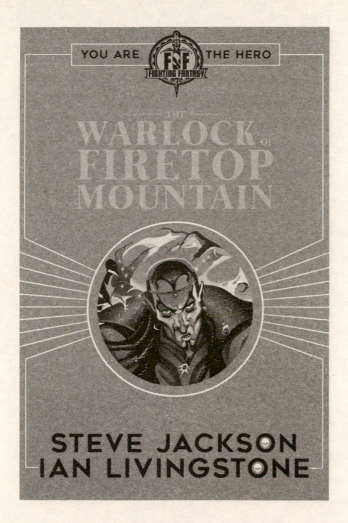

YOU ARE FIGHTING FANTASY THE HERO

THE WARLOCK OF FIRETOP MOUNTAIN

STEVE JACKSON IAN LIVINGSTONE

Are YOU brave enough to take on the monsters and the magic of Firetop Mountain?

The powerful warlock Zagor must be slain – but first you'll need to make it through the caverns of his mountain stronghold. Many adventurers before you have taken a wrong turn in the maze and perished at the hands and claws of the Warlock's gruesome servants...

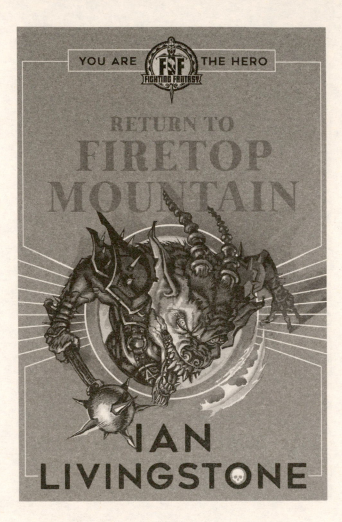

RETURN TO
FIRETOP
MOUNTAIN

IAN
LIVINGSTONE

Are YOU brave enough to face the monster-ridden labyrinth within Firetop Mountain?

The evil warlock Zagor has returned from the dead, with revenge his ultimate aim. Have you go what it takes to track him down, defeating terrifying monsters and battling dark magic on your way?

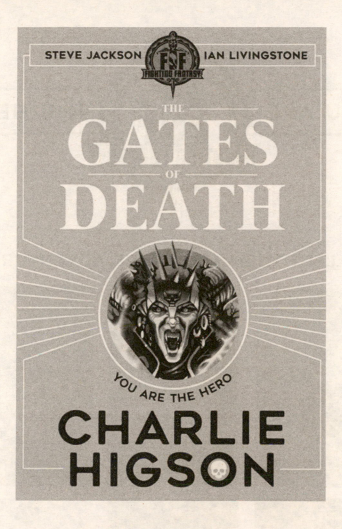

STEVE JACKSON IAN LIVINGSTONE

THE
GATES
OF
DEATH

YOU ARE THE HERO

CHARLIE
HIGSON

Every move you make could be your last...

Are YOU brave enough to face the ultimate quest? You must travel all over Allansia – including old haunts Darkwood Forest and Port Blacksand – on a dangerous mission. But what starts as a treasure hunt soon takes a darker turn, as evil sorcerer Zanbar Bone rises again. Step up, hero: it's time to fight!

YOU ARE **FIGHTING FANTASY** THE HERO

COLLECT THEM ALL, BRAVE ADVENTURER!

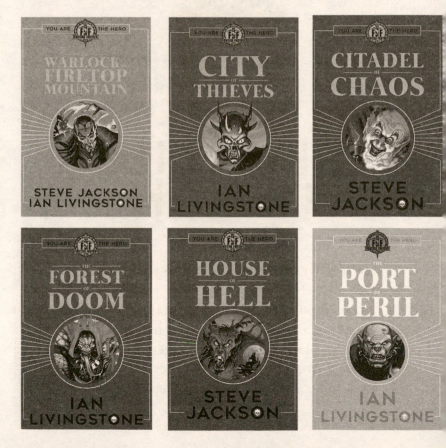

WARLOCK FIRETOP MOUNTAIN — STEVE JACKSON IAN LIVINGSTONE

CITY OF THIEVES — IAN LIVINGSTONE

CITADEL OF CHAOS — STEVE JACKSON

THE FOREST OF DOOM — IAN LIVINGSTONE

HOUSE OF HELL — STEVE JACKSON

THE PORT OF PERIL — IAN LIVINGSTONE